The Moonara 7:

Planet of Plenty

Gentil R. Cane

FOREWORD

This book is dedicated to my dear wife Sheila, who has supported me over many years in the source work from which this book is written. To my daughter Keisha, who has been the inspiration, cheerleader, and sounding board for this book. And to my son Gentil Jr., who has supported me in ways that make this book possible.

I wanted to write a book that anyone could read and enjoy. With very little violence, no cursing, and with a theme of triumph over tragic circumstances.

We live in the real world with real issues in our daily lives. This book allows us to escape to a world of fantasy, even if just to the end of its pages.

Gentil Cane

The Moonara 7: Planet of Plenty

"Booster systems," "Go." "Flight dynamics," "Go." "Guidance," "Go." "EECOM (Electrical, Environmental, and Consumables Management)," "Go." "GNC (Guidance, Navigation, and Control)," "Go." "Telemetry," "Go." "INCO (Integrated Communications)," "Go." "CAPCOM (Capsule Communicator)," "Go." "Network," "Go." "10, 9, 8, 7, 6, 5, 4, 3, 2, engine start." The latches released the spacecraft prematurely before the engines fired. This caused the heavy rocket boosters to become unsecured and unstable, falling horizontally onto the launch pad and dragging the attached spacecraft with them. In short, the launch was aborted before the engines could ignite. Emergency recovery crews rushed to get the crew out of the spacecraft and ground personnel to safety.

Almost immediately after the crew and ground personnel were safely evacuated, the impact from one of the rocket boosters cracking on the ground caused a leak. The entire spacecraft exploded minutes later, sending flames high into the sky. With the whole fuel payload ignited, the only solution was to let the boosters burn out. Although no one was seriously hurt, it was a spectacular scene—a fireball to behold! More importantly, it was a global setback for the planet.

The year is 2175, and technology has regressed by 200 years, back to 1975. It's been just six years since humans first landed on Planet Moonara (pronounced Moo-nah-rah). Fire, smoke, and molten lava simmer in the distance from Mount Moonara, but not within the crater, on the planet's dark side. Amid this chaos, a figure of great significance, the Enac Supreme, struggles to a safe place inside the crater, near death. The Enacamyte leader, a beacon of hope in these dark times, is finally discovered lying in a small cavern nearly a kilometer down. A crew member spots and rescues him, while I fly reconnaissance overhead, providing protective cover. This is our reality now—a world where advanced technology has been reduced to a shadow of its former self, and survival is a constant struggle.

But I digress. To truly understand our plight, we must start from the beginning. Join me as we uncover the events that led us to this desperate state.

Table of Contents

Chapter 1.
Say It's Not So

COLONEL JARIOUS WINDOVER SWIFT, JR.

A llow me to introduce myself. I am Colonel Jarious Windover Swift Jr., an with a story to share. Some folks call me an "OG" (Old Guard) because I still write down things that happen in my orbit. I've kept a journal since I was a young eaglet, jotting down everything. It's an old-school hobby, I guess. Maybe it's a good thing now that we've returned to New Earth. I've been in the military for 19 years, but enough about me; let's get to why we're here. It happened nearly fifty years ago. Yes, THE BIG ONE. I wasn't born yet, but my grandfather, Grandpa Jar, whom I was named after, told me the story countless times. Here's how he described it: "Accidentally, a nuclear explosion occurred due to a design flaw in a nuclear reactor, impacting five of them and a secret underground thermonuclear bomb." Even from miles away, he saw a massive explosion with giant fireballs and flashes shooting high into the air, forming a mushroom shape. It was too bright to look at directly. A deafening sound, like a sonic boom, followed as the mushroom cloud billowed smoke high into the sky. On the ground, people scattered in every direction, with nowhere to go, as the wind from the blast swept past them.

A few minutes later, he felt an intense heat. Panicked, he told his mother, Zhar. Without hesitation, she scooped him

2

up and rushed to the bomb shelter on the military base. In case you haven't guessed, my grandpa served in the military too. As he grew older, my grandpa learned more about that fateful event. He discovered that nuclear blasts send shockwaves outward at thousands of miles an hour. He also realized that it was a thermonuclear bomb with a blast yield of about 60 megatons of TNT, nearly 40 times more potent than the first nuclear bomb ever detonated. The nuclear blast was destructive, altering our planet irrevocably. Millions of humans and animals perished instantly, while countless others were deformed or mutated in various ways. Remarkably, some animals that once walked on four legs are now able to walk upright on two. Among them were cats, bears, and dogs, which, for reasons unknown to the scientific community, could suddenly speak human languages.

Scientists speculated that the chemicals released during the explosion might have caused these extraordinary changes, endowing a select few with the ability to communicate. Like me, only animals born post-catastrophe had this linguistic gift. We were not only articulate but also astonishingly intelligent, often surpassing human intelligence without formal education. We embodied values such as duty, honesty, and integrity, traits that even some humans, including those in the military, lacked.

One day, perched on a low tree limb in my favorite park, I overheard a squirrel conversing with a pony. The squirrel said, "I think it's disgraceful that animals like us, who can talk, aren't more grateful to humans. They've integrated us into their world while allowing us to remain ourselves. Sure, some humans are knuckleheads, but most are kind and accepting."

"I understand and agree," the pony replied. "But we can't ignore the history of how animals were once enslaved and treated as property. It's hard to forget that. We've made significant progress over the decades, yet there's still a long way to go." "Yeah, I get you," said the squirrel. "Anyway, I need to finish gathering nuts for the week. Catch you later."

Integrating talking animals into society took several decades. While it was relatively easy for some species, others faced greater challenges. I remember the tiger, black bear, red squirrel, rabbit, and elephant adapting quickly to their new societal roles. My black bear friend Nathan became a judge at the Planetary Council. Red squirrel Gladys and rabbit Ross, who were in my reintegration training class many years ago, now hold management positions in law enforcement. And of course, we all know the famous elephant, Stomper, a trivia game show winner and country music legend. When it was first discovered that some animals could talk, those that could have been terrified to reveal this to humans. They remembered how humans had hunted elephants for their tusks, killed red squirrels for meat, and slaughtered black bears and tigers for sport and to make rugs. They had every reason to fear the worst. Humans were initially bewildered and anxious upon learning that some animals could talk. They feared animal retribution, though a smaller percentage looked forward to the new societal order.

The other day, I overheard Gladys, a red squirrel, and Ross, a rabbit, chatting on my back deck while waiting for a food delivery. "Ross, do you think humans will ever change their attitude towards us?" Gladys asked. "I'm not sure, Gladys," Ross replied. "But our food situation has definitely improved. My mother always taught my seven siblings and me not to prejudge anyone, and to give every species a chance. So that's what I'm doing now—giving humans a chance." "I hear you, Ross, but I'll keep a close eye on them, just like I always have." Just then, the food delivery arrived, and they went their separate ways.

My family took a completely different approach. In New America, my eagle ancestors were protected, allowing us to flourish for generations. As for me, I fully support humans. My role in reintegration training is to help other animals feel more comfortable with humans despite our collective history. This isn't easy; it remains a challenge today. This has been my reality for nearly forty-three years.

To aid in the human-animal integration process, The Planetary Council established The Planet Unity Ball Games (PUBG) years ago. It's an event that uses a unique game as a unifying force. The game is a blend of soccer, rugby, and American football. The rules are simple: twenty-one players on each side on a field 200 yards long (182.8 meters). One rectangular foam object serves as the ball. The goal is to force all twenty-one of the opponent's players over your end zone marker any way you can—push, pull, drag, or carry—one at a time. Once a player crosses the opponent's end zone marker, they can no longer participate. No flying is allowed, and teams must be evenly split between humans and animals. It's a grueling sport where strength, endurance, and commitment are key to victory. The event typically lasts half a day. The losing team must feed the winning team at their quarters for a month. Teams all over New Earth eagerly anticipate the annual PUBG event. The military even has its version of PUBG, which is wildly popular among military personnel.

Speaking of species, we all must be especially aware of a particularly dangerous species, the Pi-Thar. A Pi-Thar is a human-like machine that mimics humans in every way—appearance, behavior, emotions, bodily gestures, and speech. It even surpasses human intellect. Its molecular structure, bioengineering, computer, and mechanical engineering technology have advanced so far that Pi-Thars can now teach themselves to think independently, learning from each experience. A Pi-thar's DNA is 75% to 90% machine, making it nearly impossible for humans to distinguish them from real people without DNA testing. Interestingly, a few animal species can tell the difference, which has made animals invaluable to human existence, though some humans resent them for it.

Every human and animal must undergo an annual Pi-thar exam. The DNA equivalency should be 100% human or animal but must not fall below 80%. This exam involves taking a blood sample, as mandated by international law, with results available in about five minutes. If any species' DNA is less than 80% human or animal, it is identified as a Pi-thar. These Pi-thars are immediately detained and sent to a Re-education Program, where their DNA is adjusted to an acceptable ratio. In the New United States, the government is not always honest. Some officials seek to manipulate and control Pi-thar DNA ratios for their own ambition and power.

Due to the planet's food scarcity, prospective parents must obtain government permission to conceive a child. But, despite the government's attempts to control the population, they fail to manage the Pi-thar effectively. The only species that can distinguish a human from a Pi-Thar are animals, making them invaluable to the survival of all beings.

Life around the globe is harsh. Weather patterns are unpredictable; a 15- to 20-inch rainstorm could suddenly turn into a snowstorm. Earth's fault lines are so unstable that an 8.0 earthquake could strike anywhere at any moment. Flash flooding is common everywhere, and tsunamis occur regularly. Winds can gust up to 125 miles per hour (about 201 kilometers per hour) and then die down just as quickly. The planet now consists of only 40% water, making it as valuable as gold. However, the most pressing need is a sustainable food source. Due to the planet heating up, former lakes, rivers, and entire oceans like the Atlantic, Indian, and Pacific have dried up or are polluted. While some progress has been made in water supply, it is nowhere near enough to meet the demand for planting and harvesting food for the entire planet. The privileged represent five percent of the population, while the remaining ninety-five percent live in poverty. Wars are constantly fought over food equity.

The food shortage has drastically impacted the planet's population, particularly humans, leading to a loss of creativity, impaired motor functions, and a decline in cognitive development. The young are especially vulnerable. For instance, many ten-year-old children are now at the developmental stage of five-year-olds. In short, New Earth is gradually losing its ability to progress from one generation to the next.

Necessary brain-boosting foods like green, leafy vegetables (such as kale, spinach, collards, and broccoli), fish, and berries have been depleted without any alternatives. These foods are rich in brain-healthy nutrients like vitamin K, lutein, folate, and beta-carotene.

Additionally, sources of omega-3, such as fatty fish, flaxseeds, avocados, and walnuts, essential for optimal brain function, are also scarce. Education professionals are raising the alarm about the long-term dangers of food insecurity on the planet, warning anyone who will listen. Regional conflicts are becoming more prevalent as food and water resources dwindle. The time to act decisively and aggressively is now.

Chapter 2.
Bring Back Yesterday

THE BIG ONE

There is a yearning for the days before The Big One. No more walks in the park; no more dressing comfortably in shorts, sandals, and T-shirts; no more casual weekend boat rides, as the waters everywhere are contaminated with radiation. Fishing from your favorite spot on the bank is a thing of the past. Visiting museums? Forget it, they've all been decimated and are now what we call Natural Theaters, or NTs. NTs are the new movie theaters for all things "yesterday." You pay a high fee to watch reruns of your favorite sports games and TV shows. You can also view video clips of cultural sites, such as museums and historical landmarks, from before The Big One. You can take a virtual walk in any famous park around the world or ride in a motor vehicle with four wheels on a sightseeing tour of your favorite city. Now that hovercrafts are common, tires are obsolete. Hovercrafts float just inches above the ground on stabilized air and can travel at what I consider lightning speed.

This is the world I grew up in—I have no memory of life before. Some of my closest friends are human, while some of my fiercest enemies are animals, even some of those of my species. I have a cousin, Flossy, a hawk, who despises me because I'm an eagle in the military. She says I'm being used to further disgrace and humiliate our species. She believes we have been, and continue to be, treated as second-class Planeteers (the term used for all inhabitants of New Earth). Despite these internal and external species conflicts, the planet has generally united on most of the critical issues of the day, especially those that threaten its very existence. Humans and animals have peacefully coexisted for many years, recognizing their mutual dependence for survival. Animals are integrated into every aspect of life, contributing significantly to the planet's resurgence from the brink of destruction.

Radiation contamination remains a severe issue, affecting nearly all species. Despite the passage of time, many still suffer merciful deaths due to severe deformities. These occur when a newborn, human or animal, is so malformed—such as being born without eyes, having a single eye on the side of the face, lacking a stomach, or possessing a partially developed brain—that they survive only a few minutes after birth. The silver lining in this tragic scenario is that the parents can choose to donate the unaffected organs of these newborns for research, aiding the search for a cure.

While many dwell on the past, the present and future demand immediate attention. After The Big One, the planet, now vastly different from before, is commonly referred to as "New Earth." Desperate for new food and water sources, humanity must look beyond New Earth, perhaps to other potentially habitable planets where molecules like methane, carbon dioxide, and water vapor exist in the atmosphere. These molecules often indicate the presence of life.

Chapter 3.
The Military

The Space Port is one of several strategically located facilities across the planet, designed for both military and civilian operations. I'm assigned to the Boxdale Space Port (commonly referred to as BSP) in Second Yamasville, Utah. This city got its name after "The Big One," a massive earthquake that split the state in two, creating First Utah and Second Utah. Cities in the state were now named with either "First" or "Second" in front of them to denote their location. There is at least one Space Port on every continent—New South America, New Asia, New Africa, New Australia, New Europe, New Antarctica, and New North America, where I serve. New Asia and New North America each have two Space Ports. Most military operations are humanitarian. The few wars that do occur are minor, often over food and water rights. The extensive weapon systems built before The Big One were rendered useless in its wake. The world has been forced to rely on cooperation, as no single nation could survive the catastrophe unleashed by The Big One. In a desperate bid for survival, the world's militaries merged, aiming for efficiency and effectiveness in managing the near-impossible tasks that lay ahead. Fast forward 100 years, and our planet remains ravaged by devastation. Iconic cities like New York, Paris, Rome, Moscow, Nairobi, Beijing, Doha, Johannesburg, Bergen, Melbourne, and Rio De Janeiro lie in ruins, abandoned to the elements. Squatters now inhabit these ghost cities, scraping by in a bid to survive.

The mission of the former United States Space Force (USSF), originally focused on war readiness, has fundamentally evolved to include most of the world's nations, primarily focused on logistics and research. It is now an agency that promotes peace in space and seeks ways to aid the planet in securing food and water resources. The satellites it deploys are used to locate additional water sources on New Earth and conduct research to enhance food production on the planet. Decades ago, its name was changed to the International Space Resources Agency (ISRA). ISRA serves as the lead agency for food and water exploration.

Military vehicles travel in convoys due to constant attacks from individuals desperate for food and water. One such organized group of land pirates, known as The Highway Hoods, targets critical bottlenecks on the most well-traveled highways in our area of responsibility. The Highway Hoods, led by RaphiEl, the elephant, and Shalamon, the little human, know this. That is why they attack and hijack the food convoys, taking all the Gainer Food to distribute among the people and destroying the Loser Food. While I sympathize with their plight, breaking the law is not the solution.

It is important to note that Gainer Food contains the nutrients necessary to stay healthy. Only MCC, through ISRA, has the certified list of Gainer foods, classified as a Cryptic Secret. Gainer food is grown hydroponically in a temperature-controlled, germ-free environment (since the soil is packed with radiation). A member of the Highway Hoods, formerly with MCC, knows about the existence of the Gainer Food list. That person is The Ma'am. In the New United States, the government holds an annual parade to honor military service members and veterans. Millions of people line the columns (where buildings once stood but are now just pillars of concrete and rebar) to show their appreciation. I'm not sure if the people are there for the service members or for the food they distribute at the parade. Unaware that the parade food is Loser food, the people eagerly accept it.

The transport vehicles take food and water to the heavily fortified Clearing Way Station. From there, various distribution center personnel pick up the supplies for delivery to the end consumers. I should note that sickness, disease, and deformities are everywhere. It's commonplace. Thousands of people die daily all over the world. There are no individual memorial services, as I was told there used to be before I was born. By international law, bodies are cremated within hours of death, and an official urn is presented to the next of kin. Hospitals are overrun with the sick, but treating military personnel is a top governmental priority. I saw this firsthand during my annual government-mandated health examination.

People love, honor, and respect military service members worldwide. This is because they believe the military is given superior food, referred to as Gainer food; while to the contrary they are given Loser Food, which will eventually make them sick and die. Loser food is contaminated with high levels of radiation during farming, harvesting, and preparation for sale and distribution.

Radiation is deliberately injected into a percentage of all food, aimed at killing anyone, human or animal, who consumes it. One serving will slowly but surely lead to death within two weeks. The purpose of Loser Food is to reduce the population, targeting the poorest and most vulnerable. Rank-and-file military personnel believe they are performing an honorable service for the people. However, the top military officers at Mission Central Command (MCC) are fully aware of the truth. MCC brass controls and directs this sinister operation. It remains unclear whether the Loser Food situation is unique to New America or if it spans the entire planet.

There is an antidote to eating Loser Food if injected directly into the bloodstream within 72 hours. Our very own "The Ma'am" (more about her later) was part of the MCC research team that developed and operationalized this antidote a few years ago. She left MCC after advocating for its widespread distribution to any human or animal in need. Her recommendation was denied. All antidotes are stored at MCC and are intentionally kept in short supply.

Chapter 4.
Who's Who

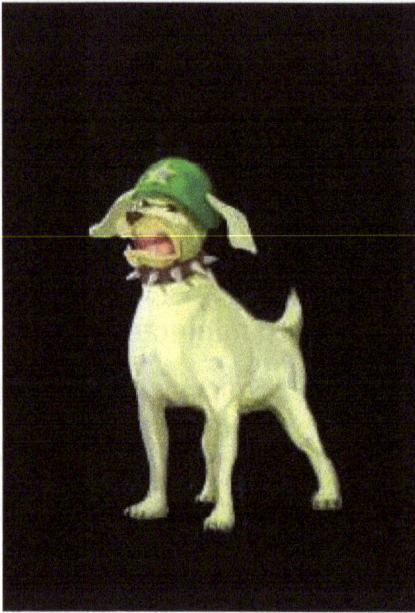

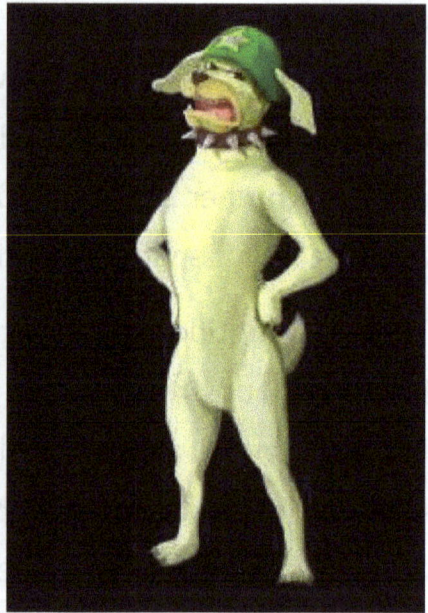

GENERAL SHARTANKARUS BOXDALE (AKA "TANK")

N ow, more about me. I am a military brat, thanks to my father, Windover Swift, and my Grandpa Jar, whom I told you about earlier. Growing up, we moved around a lot, so most of my worldview is through the lens of the military. I hold a strong belief in God, country, and family. My wife, Saba'ta, is a falcon from the nation of Cywaneeze. In our world, international law considers humans and animals equal, though many humans still believe they are superior. I serve as a Reconnaissance Specialist. My job is first to enter any mission operations area, assess the conditions, and report to the Mission Command Center (MCC) through the Space Port Commander. I work closely with a small group of military professionals. We are like a family, with all the camaraderie and disputes that come with it. However, we share a common commitment to our assigned mission and a deep respect for authority and the chain of command. We serve under the command of General Shartankarus Boxdale, known to us as "The Tank" (though never to his face). Those under his command call him "General." He is a career military officer with over 41 years of service, and over the years, he has been a part of too many military campaigns to number. He is a highly competent and decorated space pilot and navigator. General Boxdale is as challenging, determined, and demanding as they come, with an attitude to match. When he gets excited and animated about something, he stands upright on his two hind legs, but you know he means business when he drops to all four paws, barking out orders or rallying the troops. The stakes are higher than ever, and every mission counts. Our next move could determine the fate of not just our team, but our entire world. General Boxdale has a chip on his shoulder because, according to him, there's no reason he shouldn't have been promoted to two-star General by now. He's been the Commander at Space Port for so long that MCC named the facility after him: Boxdale Space Port (BSP). He and I understand each other well, having worked together for fifteen years. Most everyone else is afraid of him. I was in the fitness center, strengthening my connecting wing muscles, when the General came in for his daily workout. Sergeant Z was finishing up his fitness routine. "Good morning, sir," I greeted the General. "Morning," he replied. "Any word on our next mission?" I asked. "No, you know MCC takes its own sweet time with these things," he said. "Understood," I responded.

The General walked over to the free weights where Sergeant Z had just finished. "Good morning, General. Need a spotter today?" asked Sergeant Z. "Nah, Sarge, I got it. Not going to lift much. Not feeling it today," the General replied. "Understood," said Sergeant Z as he picked up his towel and headed for the showers. The General and I were now alone in the fitness center. He looked around to make sure no one else was present. I knew what was coming next: the issue about his promotion. "Win," he said, using my nickname short for Windover, my first name, "there's no good reason MCC shouldn't have released my promotional orders by now. The Universal Council has already approved the slate." I nodded in agreement. Another person entered the fitness center, and our conversation halted. Two good human friends, Sergeant Zinginfus and The Ma'am, who also serve with me at the BSP facilities.

SERGEANT ZINGINFUS

Sergeant Zinginfus (we call him Sergeant Z) hails from HeBerzon, but he and his younger sister, Tolay, came to the New United States with their Uncle Roz when he was three years old, after their parents' tragic deaths—his mother during childbirth and his father from an infection caused by The Big One. At just three years old, Sergeant Z became the father figure to his sister. Sergeant Z is the disciplinarian of our small group, a hard-charging infantryman through and through. He ensures we follow orders from MCC relayed by General Boxdale, instilling confidence in every mission, no matter how daunting. As our Weapons Certification expert, Sergeant Z is especially knowledgeable about our primary weapon, the Weapon Of Laughter, or WOL. The WOL triggers specific sensory mechanisms in the body upon contact, causing uncontrollable laughter. This results in an immediate drop in heart rate, blood pressure, muscular tension, and stress hormones. The WOL emits 1 to 3 kilojoules of energy, with each kilojoule taking about a second to release. While a standard WOL burst is set to 1 kilojoule, a 3-kilojoule burst for three seconds or more can fatally overload the heart. Sergeant Z harbors feelings for The Ma'am (more on her later) but adheres strictly to military fraternization rules, keeping his distance. He confided this to me, the group's unofficial confidant, as no one dares approach General Boxdale despite his open-door policy. Sergeant Z also manages our convoy Security, successfully keeping the Highway Hoods at bay. As our physical training instructor, he keeps us in peak condition. Misuse a WOL or gain an ounce of fat, and you'll hear from him loud and clear.

Sergeant Z is a good friend of Sergeant Paw, who drives him crazy with his antics and pranks. I was the Duty Officer for the week, responsible for overseeing all weapons qualifications at the WOL and Munitions Range. Naturally, Sergeant Z conducted the qualifications, and Sergeant Paw was among those scheduled to qualify today.

Before the qualifications started, Sergeant Paw strolled over to where Sergeant Z and I were standing. He saluted me and said, "Good afternoon, Colonel." I returned the salute and replied, "Hello, Sergeant Paw. Still a Sergeant today, right?" He laughed, "Yes, sir. It's been a year since I was re-promoted." Turning to Sergeant Z, he asked, "Can I see you for a minute?" Sergeant Z glanced at me and said, "I'll be right back, sir." They walked a few meters away, close enough for me to overhear part of their conversation. Sergeant Paw asked, "Man, can you lend me some money until payday? I want to ask Private Prissy out this weekend." I couldn't hear Sergeant Z's response, but I saw him pull out his wallet and hand Sergeant Paw some money. I did catch Sergeant Z's final words: "This is the last time, man. You still owe me from before.

Now, let me tell you about my favorite human, The Ma'am. While her official professional title is Nutritional Scientist, she is much more than that to all of us. She holds the rank of Captain, and her name is Emil Strassenborgg, but to us, she has the stature of a general. She is a workaholic who finds immense pleasure in searching for alternative food sources for the planet. She mentors Lieutenant Gloria Jancedar, a trusted research assistant. The Ma'am holds an M.D. degree from a prestigious medical school in Germany. Her parents immigrated to the New United States when she was young. Although she spent her formative years in the US, she returned to Germany to study medicine, focusing on how food interacts with human and animal bodies.

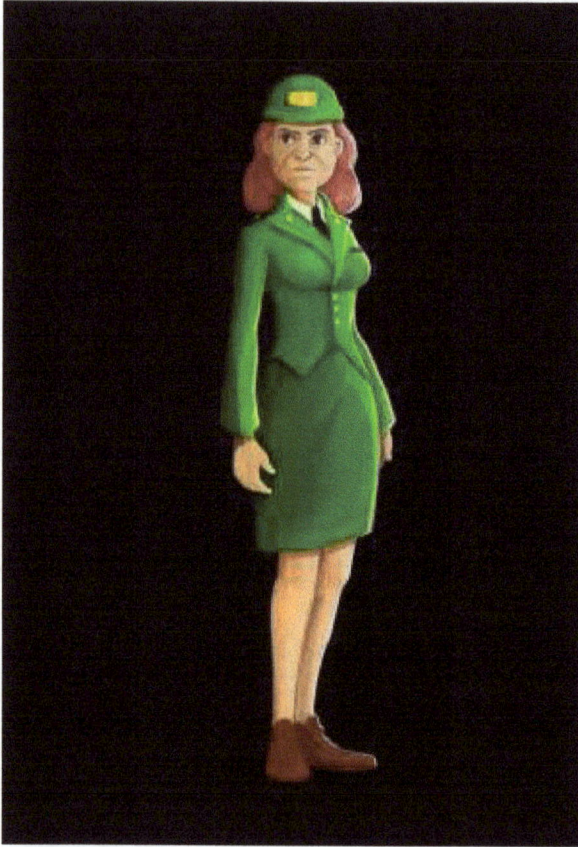

CAPTAIN EMIL STRASSENBORGG (AKA THE MA' AM)

The Ma'am is beloved and respected by everyone in our working group, earning her the title. She is incredibly intelligent, empathetic, and deeply cares about others, especially those with fewer resources. Quietly, The Ma'am respects and admires General Boxdale for his courage, conviction, and leadership. It was an early Saturday evening, around 1900 hours, and we were playing our usual digital card game at Tank's quarters—just him and me. There were three firm, successive knocks on the door. After about fifteen seconds, there were three more. General Boxdale was annoyed. He got up, went to the door, and there stood The Ma'am. She was the Duty Officer of the week. "I have a Cryptic Secret message for your eyes only sir, and I am to wait for a reply," she said. Still annoyed but trying to be professional, General Boxdale took the document and replied, "Captain Strassenborgg, would you like to come in?" "Yes, sir," she said. The General quickly moved to a private area to read the message, while The Ma'am waited. As she stood there, I asked, "How is the food research coming along? Do you expect a breakthrough soon? "It's not going as well as I hoped, but we're trying new formulas in hopes of a breakthrough," she replied. General Boxdale returned and handed The Ma'am the document folder. "Thank you, sir," she said, turning to leave. General Boxdale followed her to the door. After she left, I said to General Boxdale, "Tank, she admires and respects you, I can tell." "Win, I'm just trying to do my best with what I've got," he said. "Understood," I replied, and we both laughed and continued our digital card game.

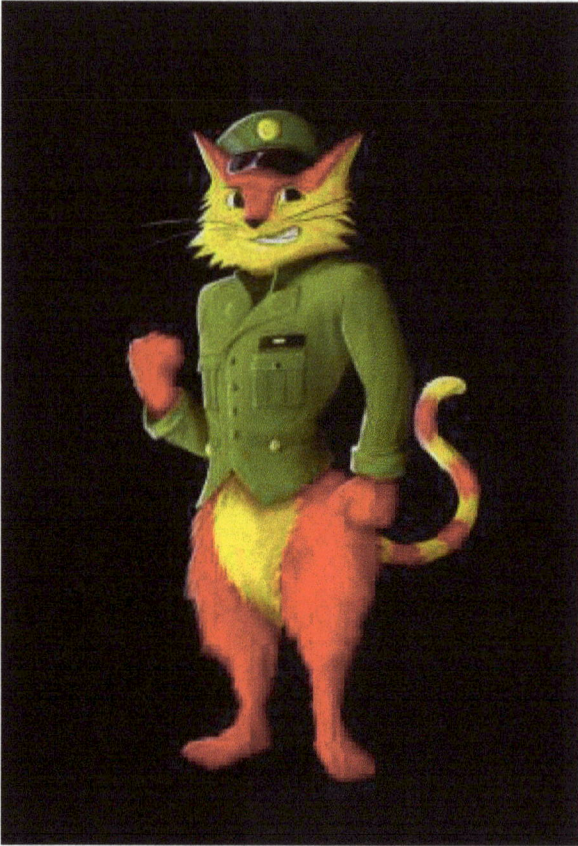

SERGEANT FELESIOUS PAW

Switching to a lighter note, that brings to mind Sergeant Felesious Paw. He's defensive about his first name because it sounds like a queen's, not a king's name, but he's quick to assert his masculine tomcat ways. If the average cat has nine lives, Sergeant Paw has twice that many. He's highly proficient as a Spacecraft Navigator. With no active mission, he's always at the spacecraft simulator, honing his skills. But his antics often get him into trouble, driving

SERGEANT WADDLES

Sergeant Z crazy. He's the comedian of the group, having been in the military for ten years and disciplined three times for his pranks. Recently, he was promoted back to sergeant—again.

He loves telling practical jokes, but they don't amuse me. For instance, he once said, "I was so upset when I found out that I had been cloned, I was beside myself." Not only was this joke unfunny to me, but it also reminded me of Pi-thars, a serious matter. Another joke he told was, "Did you hear about the person who got hit with a can of soda? They're okay. It was just a soft drink."

Sergeant Paw loved everything about spacecraft. He also had a soft spot for Private Prissy. Once, to impress her, he took an unauthorized flight in a space pod, showing off his flying skills. His daring stunt earned him a disciplinary Article 165 and a demotion back to corporal. But he didn't mind; Private Prissy had enjoyed his display of piloting prowess. When it came to navigation, Sergeant Paw was the go-to expert. Sergeant Paw and Private Prissy both served at the BSP (more about her later). Everyone there knew about Sergeant Paw's admiration for Private Prissy.

A duck without much water is an unhappy duck, and Sergeant Waddles often felt this way. I serve with Sergeant Waddles at the BSP. He is the newest member of our group, having been assigned here less than a year ago. He's so new that I don't even know his first name. He replaced Sergeant Blutenfield as the BSP Munitions Specialist. From what I've learned about him, he's a very serious-minded service member, always ready for the next mission. I once overheard him telling General Boxdale that even though he occasionally wears goggles, he has perfect 20/20 vision and is fully capable of carrying out any assignment. In his off-duty hours, Sergeant Waddles can be found swimming in the Aquatics Dome, an internal structure specifically built to test ways to improve the planet's water quality. There, he can swim naturally in purified, radiation-free water. Due to the radiation-infested waters on the planet, he rarely gets to use his natural swimming skills. Sergeant Waddles has become friends with Private Prissy, as she is assigned to the Aquatics Dome as her duty station.

Another day of practice landings at the Aquatic Dome. I ran into Sergeant Waddles, whom I hadn't seen in a while. He greeted me with a grin, "Colonel, I guess you've been busy with reconnaissance missions?" I shook my head. "No, Sergeant, just a lot of trial runs. How have you been?" Before he could respond, Private Prissy interrupted, "Good morning, sir." I returned her greeting, and Sergeant Waddles added, "I'm fine, sir. Just need to get my swims in." Turning to Private Prissy, he asked, "Hey, Missie, are you going to that social tonight?" She hesitated. "I'm not sure."

It was clear they were good friends, and I took that as my cue to leave. It was nice seeing the younger generation so active and carefree. Private Prissy, or Private Missie as some called her, was one of the service members who served with me at the BSP as well. As a Water Quality Specialist, her military entrance scores were off the charts. Though quiet by nature, she would light up when discussing anything related to water. She worked well with her peers and superiors, though she was often a loner. In her off-duty hours, she could usually be found stargazing at the observatory, always dreaming of space. General Boxdale mentioned she'd only been in the military for about a year. That's when I learned her first name was Melissa. She had spent over three and a half years at the local university pursuing Environmental Studies. With just six months left to graduate, she was forced to drop out to fulfill a promise she made to her older sister—to care for her ten-year-old niece, Se-rye. Her sister had passed away two years ago from an inoperable, metastasized kidney disease. Struggling to find work, Missie joined the military to provide for her niece. Now, she's also taking online classes to complete her Skills Certification, formerly known as a bachelor's degree.

PRIVATE MELISSA PRISSY

A carnivore at heart, Private Prissy loves almost any seafood you set before her. She has a particular fondness for salmon, and as I mentioned before, Sergeant Paw likes Private Prissy very much. Knowing her preference, he often brings her salmon. While Private Prissy likes Sergeant Paw too, it's only as a good friend. She thinks Sergeant Z is the best sergeant in the world and respects him greatly. One thing Sergeant Paw has in his favor is that Private Prissy, being traditionally reared in her clowder, believes a suitor should seek her out. She pretends to pay little attention to Sergeant Paw and, when asked about him, says, "He's just a good friend. Besides, I need to finish my coursework and learn as much as possible from Captain Strassenborgg." The Captain has been mentoring her at the Aquatic Dome for some time. I stopped by the Aquatic Dome to practice pinpoint landings in the water and saw Lieutenant Jancedar and Private Prissy conversing with The Ma'am. I overheard Lieutenant Jancedar say, "Since this is my last day, may I leave a little earlier?" The Ma'am replied, "Of course. You have been a great asset to the BSP in general and our food and water research efforts in particular. Thank you." Private Prissy added, "While I haven't known you long, it has been nice working with you. Good luck with your next assignment."

Lieutenant Jancedar departed while The Ma'am and Private Prissy continued their conversation. I took flight for my first practice run. After completing it, I returned to find them still talking. I greeted them, and they acknowledged me with morning pleasantries. Then The Ma'am said, "Colonel Swift, do you know my newest assistant, Private Prissy? She's a very bright young woman, and I'm expecting a lot from her." I replied, "No, I don't believe I have had the pleasure. You're going to find us a sustainable food source, right?" I looked directly at Private Prissy. "Sir," she said, "I will do my best." "It's time for us to wrap up things around here, Colonel. See you, sir," the Ma'am said. They walked away, and I prepared for my second practice run.

It was mid-August, a few days before General Boxdale's birthday, when the XO (Executive Officer) invited the entire BSP staff to the Gathering Hall for a surprise celebration. This was the social event I overheard Private Prissy and Sergeant Waddles discussing earlier. Typically, officers don't mingle socially with non-officers, but given our small group, all 50 or so of us were invited. Can you believe it? Even Rascal was invited (more about him later).

That night, I walked around the room, talking to everyone and trying to make them feel welcome. I saw Sergeants Z, Paw, and Waddles huddled near the refreshment table, talking. I walked over, and we greeted each other. At that moment, Private Prissy entered the Hall, and Sergeant Paw immediately said, "Wow, doesn't she look gorgeous." Sergeant Waddles replied, "She looks all right." Laughing, Sergeant Paw responded, "Little duck, you don't know what you're talking about. That is perfection." I exchanged some general conversation with Sergeant Paw about his navigation training before leaving the group.

Chapter 5.
Addressing The Problem

One week before my birthday, a chilly September evening enveloped me as I returned home from a reconnaissance night flight. The emergency alarm on my communicator jolted me into action. With a swift wave of my hand over the device, I checked the time: 21:27 hours (9:27 pm). The message flashed in cryptic letters: CRYPTIC SECRET. Proceed to Berth 44 immediately. Berth 44 is a large, now grounded super tanker converted into warehouse space and sleeping quarters for special operations.

Rushing out again, I donned my wing protectors in one fluid motion, my mind racing with questions. It had been months since my communicator last sounded with such urgency, and then it was merely a test message. What could this call mean on New Earth? Finally, I arrived at Berth 44, and being the second team member to arrive, I found General Boxdale already there, waiting. Over the next few minutes, our team of seven assembled at the entrance of Berth 44, each having received the same message. Silently exchanging glances, we watched as the titanium entrance door slowly descended. Upon reaching the ground, a bold red display flashed "ENTER" on its side panel. With cautious steps, led by General Boxdale, we entered. Inside, an elevator awaited us, its doors sliding open as we approached. Stepping inside, the elevator plunged downwards, the descent feeling interminable despite lasting only fifteen seconds.

The doors slid open to silence. For what seemed an eternity, nothing stirred. Then, a commanding artificial female voice filled the cabin. "Detach and place all communication devices in the receptacle on the wall." A panel extended, and we complied, but the tension was palpable.

Exiting the elevator, we stepped into a vast open bay that stretched before us, revealing a colossal spacecraft resting horizontally on the ground — the most magnificent I had ever seen. As we marveled at its presence, a two-star General materialized and gestured for us to follow him. We obeyed, winding our way to what resembled a briefing room. Seated, we awaited further instructions as the two-star General departed, leaving us in suspense for what felt like an eternity.

After what seemed like ages, a three-star General entered the room. "You have passed your first test," he declared cryptically. Confused, we later discovered that our endurance through the prolonged wait had been a test of stress tolerance, and patience. The three-star general, who I now know is General Verdy, began to speak. He said we each had been under observation for months to determine our psychological and physical fitness for a special mission to other planets to look for alternative food sources. He stated that by a random process, the New United States had been selected as the lead nation to represent the world in its quest to find an alternative food source. He further stated that MCC, in collaboration with ISRA, had appointed him to oversee the mission. But before discussing further details, he would need to interview each of us individually.

After a day-long interview process, beginning the following morning, we all reconvened at Berth 44. General Verdy informed the group that all seven of us had agreed to be part of the mission, allowing him to share more details. He explained that each of our technical skills was essential for the mission's success and that we could be away for up to a year and a half, depending on what we found and on which planet. From previous missions, he noted that our nearest planet, Moonara, did not appear to have the alternative food sources we needed, so we would skip researching it for now. Instead, General Verdy stated that the decision had been made to investigate three planets in our galaxy: C-1954, A-1978, and N-1990.

General Verdy informed us about a secret weapon developed to counteract the Pi'thar, known as the "Brill." It's an Artificial Intelligence (AI) designed to resemble a human, assigned to our mission. This cutting-edge model, named Rascal, is the latest in AI technology. Built from a titanium inner frame with nanometer-scale computer technology beyond human comprehension, Rascal has an outer layer that mimics human flesh, muscles, and bones.

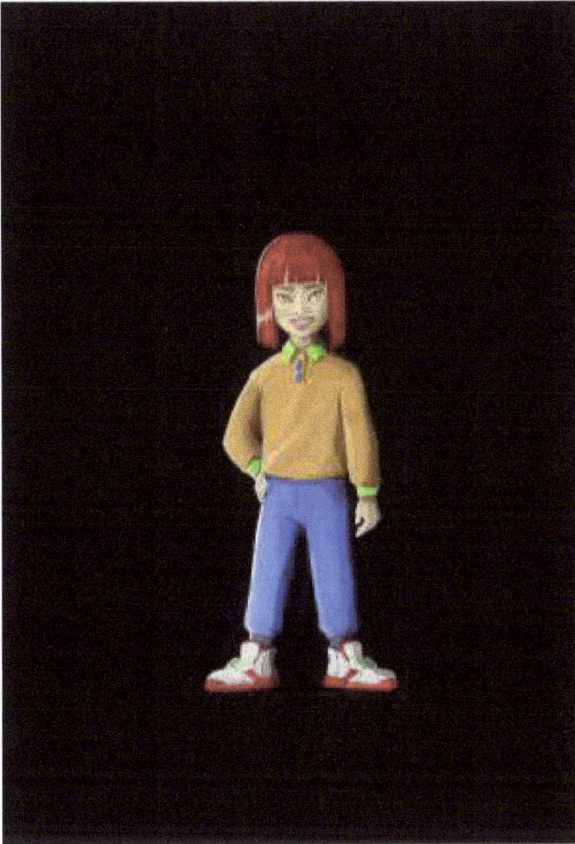

RASCAL

The name "Brill" reflects its exceptional intelligence, design, memory, thought processes, emotional intelligence, and independent thinking capacity, which surpass human capabilities. General Boxdale later assigned Rascal a male gender. Specifically crafted for our mission, Rascal's facial features sometimes appear feminine. The AI was named Rascal due to its embedded, harmless mischievous coding, designed to lighten the mood and boost morale during long journeys.

Rascal resembles a twelve-year-old boy/girl depending on perception. Standing at 1.37 meters tall (4.5 feet) and weighing just over 44.4 kilograms (98 lbs.), Rascal has smooth, light tan skin. His eyes are slanted like a cat's, slightly upward, with yellowish-green irises sporting a vertical disc shape and a black outer ring, giving them an intense gaze that Private Prissy jokingly compares to her own. He sports a pug nose, lips with a hint of collagen, striking red eyebrows matching his hair, straight red hair falling just above his shoulders with bangs, and a slender build. His attire consists of non-military unisex clothing – casual jeans and a colorful collared top with two buttons – paired with stylish, colorful sneakers. Rascal frequently laughs, revealing perfectly aligned, pearly white teeth. He embodies what I'd describe as a universal humanoid.

Rascal is a unique blend of 50% machine and 50% human DNA, with a coding that sets him apart from standard AI like Pi-thars. Despite his mechanical nature, he experiences human emotions—laughter, tears, and empathy—though he's not truly human. Programmed with 50,000 jokes for all occasions and 30,000 harmless pranks, he possesses a distinctive laugh that starts as a gentle chuckle, building into a crescendo that echoes through the room, his face maintaining an impassive expression as he gazes towards the ceiling. Designed to pilot spacecraft and equipped with an encyclopedic knowledge of every planet in our solar system, Rascal responds to voice commands, prioritizing General Boxdale's instructions over those of Sergeant Paw in case of conflicting orders.

We were eager to commence our mission, none more so than Private Prissy, for whom this opportunity was a lifelong dream. With a year to prepare, we were assigned to our new living quarters. Thanks to special permission from MCC, Private Prissy's ten-year-old niece, Se-rye, would join her on the mission—a decision reached after intense debates and several meetings, ultimately approved due to their unique circumstances.

Chapter 6.
The Journey Begins

T raining for the interplanetary mission kicked off immediately, with the launch date set for September 27th the following year. The mission? To explore distant planets for potential human habitation with food and water sources for New Earth. Named Genesys, the spacecraft symbolized a groundbreaking endeavor, boasting a sleek, royal blue design that exuded aerodynamic perfection. It could launch vertically or horizontally and land gently, akin to a hot air balloon descending with a parachute. Its oversized portholes offered unparalleled views of the cosmos, while a four-layered nose-coned heat and light shield expanded when activated.

Genesys's solar panels were adjustable at various angles, ensuring optimal alignment with the sun for unlimited energy. Equipped with breakaway rocket boosters and a large onboard escape pod capable of accommodating the entire crew, Genesys was a marvel of single-compartment spacecraft design, made possible by years of meticulous research and development. Another version was in production, but Genesys, the pioneer, was about to undergo field testing. The training regimen was rigorous, testing our emotions and resilience. As a team, we grew interdependent, learning to rely on each other amidst the demanding preparations. Even Se-rye, our young crewmate, received specialized training in educational studies and space operations, preparing meticulously for her role in the upcoming journey.

The mission required us to travel first to planet C-1954, followed by planets A-1978 and N-1990. No human or animal had ever visited these three planets, and little was known about them. Our training schedule was designed to maximize our time together. Sometimes, during our meals, we would speculate about finding abundant sources of food and water on each planet, discussing which one we would recommend to MCC.

We made every effort to spend our precious free time with our loved ones. My wife, Saba'ta, would often cry when we were together. She understood the nobility and necessity of my mission but would dearly miss me. We've been together for so long, and this separation would be our longest yet. Though I tried to reassure her, I felt the weight of our parting as keenly as she did. With her exceptional flying skills, she mentioned that when she felt lonely for me, she would fly as high as possible, just to feel a little closer to me.

As the training dragged on, we grew increasingly anxious about the journey—not the mission itself, but the anticipation for it to begin. One morning, about two months before our launch date, we arrived to find our spacecraft had been rolled out near the launch pad. Excitement buzzed through all of us; it was all we could talk about for some time. From then on, there were pre-checks, protocols, and more to complete. We didn't mind, though; it was finally feeling real. Due to the uncertainties ahead, our weapons training became intense. Our primary weapon, the Weapon of Laughter (WOL), emits a short burst of intense light that envelops the entire body, accompanied by a sound resembling frying bacon. Its effect induces uncontrollable laughter in the target, making them easier to manage. The laughter lasts approximately two hours, sufficient to subdue the target. Extended use in longer bursts can be fatal, causing cardiac arrest. There are both short-stock and long-stock versions of the WOL.

Sergeant Z and the Tank himself were part of the research and development team that designed it. I refer to this weapon as the WOLR (Weapon Of Last Resort). It turns out the WOL is particularly effective against human and animal species, especially those that are one hundred percent Pithar. Just one month before the launch date, The Ma'am came down with influenza. We were unsure if the physicians would clear her for the mission, considering her critical role. However, two weeks before launch, she received clearance, much to our relief. Throughout this time, one thing that bound us together was Se-rye. She was not only lovable but also incredibly cute. Her youthful charm and personality refocused us all on the mission's broader purpose—for her generation and beyond.

Chapter 7.
The Big Bang and the Departure

Finally, the day of departure had arrived. We were all filled with nervous excitement. The physicians reassured us that elevated heart rates were normal under the circumstances. Se-rye, always the composed one, assured us adults that everything would be fine. Her calm demeanor stood out amidst our jittery anticipation.

Our mission, aimed at locating potential food and water sources, could last well beyond a year. This duration hinges on whether we utilize the scalar drive as an auxiliary propulsion system to boost our speed and on our success in finding these essential resources. General Boxdale harbors reservations about scalar drive technology due to its checkered history of failures. Delays in locating and analyzing potential resources found might prolong our stay on the planet.

Genesys's objective is to establish an orbit that leverages the gravitational forces of both Earth and the Sun, ensuring a stable trajectory around the Sun. Genesys will orbit the Sun similarly to the unmanned James Webb Space Telescope (JWST) of the early 21st century, stationed 1.5 million kilometers away from New Earth at Lagrange Point L2. In contrast, its predecessor, the Hubble Space Telescope, orbited Old Earth. Genesys will maintain its orbit around the Sun at a distance of 3.2 million kilometers (2 million miles) from New Earth, positioned at the Third Lagrange point (L3). This unique orbit allows Genesys and its mini-JWST satellite to remain aligned with Earth's movement around the Sun, protected by sun shields from the Sun's intense radiation and heat. This alignment ensures a stable trajectory in sync with New Earth's orbit.

Scalar drive technology harnesses solar radiation to propel spacecraft at speeds exceeding 2,092 kilometers (1,300 miles) per minute. Despite its integration into Genesys's systems, it will not serve as the primary power source due to past catastrophic failures. Also, unlike most interplanetary flights of our day, we will not be put into a hibernated state. Technology has advanced to the point where we will take certain prescribed medications to avoid the everyday hazards the body would suffer on such an extended mission. However, we each had assigned daily tasks to perform as directed by MCC.

As we sat on the launch pad, conducting the final checks, General Boxdale reminded us of what was at stake. This mission could change the future of both human and animal-kind. At that moment, he was the epitome of leadership. I felt a surge of patriotism for my country and our planet. We were ready for anything, and I sensed my crewmates, even little Se-rye, felt the same.

We were secured in The Genesys, our planned new beginning, anxiously awaiting launch for the most critical mission to ensure the survival of our world, New Earth. The seven of us, plus our AI assistant, Rascal, were poised for history.

From MCC, the Test Director's voice cut through the tension, initiating the Launch Status Check. "Booster systems," "Go." "Flight dynamics," "Go." "Guidance," "Go." "EECOM (Electrical, Environmental, and Consumables Management)," "Go." "GNC (Guidance, Navigation, and Control)," "Go." "Telemetry," "Go." "INCO (Integrated Communications)," "Go." "CAPCOM (Capsule Communicator)," "Go." "Network," "Go." The status checks continued, and my mind wandered to what lay ahead.

The countdown began, "…8, 7, 6, 5, 4, 3…" My mind went blank. The next thing I remembered was waking up in the medical center two days later. They told me that the latches releasing the spacecraft did so prematurely before the engines fired. This caused the heavy rocket boosters to become unsecured and unstable, falling horizontally onto the launch pad and dragging the attached spacecraft with them. In short, the launch was aborted before the engines could ignite. Emergency recovery crews had rushed to get us out of the spacecraft.

Almost immediately after the crew and ground personnel were safely evacuated, the impact from one of the rocket boosters cracking on the ground caused a leak. Minutes later, the entire spacecraft exploded, sending flames high into the sky. With the entire fuel payload ignited, the only solution was to let the boosters burn out. Although no one was seriously hurt, they said it was a spectacular scene—a fireball to behold! More importantly, it was a global setback for the planet.

Fortunately, New Australia had commissioned a prototype spacecraft similar to the Genesys, scheduled to be operational in a few weeks. This second food and water exploratory vehicle was now approved as the replacement for our mission. It was flown to New America for final launch preparations.

At the next crew meeting, General Boxdale informed us that the MCC, in consultation with ISRA, had set the new launch date for December 25th, just three months away. I had some reservations about the date due to my religious beliefs but kept them to myself. Although the crew was physically fine, we were required to undergo extensive psychological and emotional examinations. The second launch was named the Human and Animal Resource Mission, code-named HARM. Thus, the spacecraft was called The HARM.

Training for the upcoming HARM mission's second launch attempt began in earnest. The excitement among the crew was palpable. Ninety days of intense training flew by, and the launch was only a week away. We took a few days off to enjoy the holidays with our families. Sergeant Paw asked Private Prissy if he could spend time off with her, but she declined. So, he took Rascal home with him. We returned to BSP on December 23rd to make final preparations for our Christmas Day launch.

In the weeks leading up to the launch, General Boxdale met with us regularly to assess our readiness. Two weeks before the launch, one such meeting revealed some warranted apprehension among the crew. I remember the General addressing us, "If you're feeling anxious or afraid, raise your hand." Rascal, always the joker, quickly raised both hands. Everyone laughed. To ease our nerves, the General raised his hand and said, "That close call during the last launch attempt was tough. It's natural to feel anxious about doing it again." Reluctantly, perhaps fearing condemnation, each crew member raised their hand one by one. The General then shared a story from his combat days many years ago. We laughed hysterically when he admitted that he was so scared, he soiled himself and couldn't change immediately.

Our second launch date had finally arrived. The countdown began, and my heart raced with a mix of anxiety and excitement. Sitting atop The HARM, I felt the powerful engines roar to life, ready to lift us into our journey. It was hard not to think about what had happened on the launch pad a few months earlier. We were all feeling a double dose of anxiety. As we went through the protocols and waited for the launch, General Boxdale muted the audio access for MCC and asked each of us how we were really feeling. He wanted to gauge our anxiety levels for himself.

Private Prissy was the first to speak. "I'd be lying if I said I wasn't nervous. But I'm still excited about the chance to complete what we started." Sergeant Waddles added, "We went through some tough challenges during our first mission. While I'm apprehensive about today's launch, I'm excited to be here with all of you." The Ma'am responded confidently, "Heck yeah, I'm anxious about this launch. But I've been working towards this moment my entire career. Bringing sustainable food and water sources to our planet trumps any personal fears I might have." "If this is the hill I'm flying on and dying on, so be it: shaking wings, nervous stomach, and all," I said. Sergeant Paw grinned, "I've got nine lives, so I have a few to spare for you guys. Count me in as being uneasy about this launch." "I'm not scared at all," quipped Sergeant Z. "I'm terrified, but you won't see it. We've got a mission to accomplish." Rascal, ever the joker, said, "I'm not nervous at all. I have no apprehensions. I'm completely fine with this second launch. General, permission to leave The HARM now?" We all burst out laughing, lightening the mood. General Boxdale nodded, "It's a natural response to feel what you've just shared. If you didn't, something would be awfully wrong. Our goal is to be committed to the mission despite our fears or doubts.

Now, let's get on with it." With that, he unmuted the MCC audio.

On the second launch attempt of The HARM, something extraordinary occurred—a total solar eclipse. As you might know, this phenomenon happens when the moon passes between the Earth and the sun, casting a shadow and plunging our world into an eerie daytime darkness. In our region, such an event is rare, occurring only once every 300 years. But on our second launch date, the eclipse arrived 150 years ahead of schedule. Despite the ominous timing, there were no significant safety concerns, so the launch proceeded as planned. Still, this unexpected cosmic event cast a shadow over our mission, both literally and figuratively. Had we foreseen the string of unanticipated events that would follow, we might have reconsidered our departure date from New Earth.

Chapter 8.
The Unexpected

Instantly, it felt as if we were already a kilometer above New Earth. The next thing I remember is the spacecraft seemingly floating on nothing. We had passed the Karman Line, about 100 kilometers (62 miles) above sea level. The mission had officially begun; gravity had given way to weightlessness. As we ascended, burned, and jettisoned our rocket boosters, we had just achieved microgravity, and our spacecraft positioned itself horizontally.

Through the portholes, we watched as the planet began to darken, rotating from one continent to the next until the entire surface was cloaked in night. Suddenly, a ball of fire erupted from the New European continent. Despite our satellite network still being operational, our attempts to contact MCC for more information were met with silence.

I made my way to the navigation compartment to see General Boxdale. As I entered, I heard a voice from MCC's communications channel say, "It's bad, really bad all over," in a weak, trembling tone. The voice continued, "Going to shelter," before cutting off abruptly. General Boxdale repeatedly called out, "Mission Central, can you hear me?" but received no response. We had no idea what had happened, but whatever it was, it was catastrophic and global. The room fell silent as we all tried to process what we had just witnessed. General Boxdale broke the silence. "Whatever happened on New Earth is beyond our control. Let's focus on our mission. I'll brief you as soon as I hear any updates." With that, we all dispersed to our duty stations. "What could it possibly be?" I wondered, as hours passed without any word on the situation. Then, around 1600 hours, General Boxdale called us back to the navigation compartment—our designated gathering place. His face had a grave expression as he began to speak.

"I have bad news to report. An accident occurred at one of New Europe's largest nuclear reactor sites. There are 15 reactors at the site, and all fail-safe measures have been compromised. Nine reactors have been breached, releasing radioactive contamination into the atmosphere. To make matters worse, a significant portion of the contamination has entered the jet stream, spreading westward. In a matter of days, the entire planet will be affected." A quiet, solemn mood fell over the room. We were left in stunned silence, each of us grappling with the enormity of the disaster unfolding below us.

General Boxdale continued, "Each of your families has been moved to secure underground shelters built after the Big One. So that's some good news. As more information comes in, I will share it with you." With that, we all returned to our assigned tasks. That evening, as I headed back to my quarters, my mind drifted to my days as a young eaglet in school, learning about the aftermath of the Big One. The devastation it caused—radioactive debris leading to severe skin burns, eye damage, radiation sickness, cancer, and death—was unimaginable. The nuclear explosion's lingering effects still haunt our climate today.

In New Earth's current fragile state, another release of radioactive particles could trigger a "nuclear winter," much like the Big One did, causing global temperatures to plummet and annihilate humans, animals, and crops for years. I recalled my grandpa's stories about the Big One's aftermath: temperatures dropping by 50 to 75 degrees worldwide, wiping out crops, and rendering the soil barren.

This ongoing struggle for food and water is why our mission must succeed.

Nearly three days after launch, as we began the slingshot maneuver around Planet Moonara, Se'rye spotted a red ray of light. "Do you see that?" she asked. We all confirmed we did. The light persisted for several minutes before fading away. What could it be? I wondered. What purpose might it serve? There was no time to investigate further; we had more pressing onboard tasks. We tried to contact MCC to see if they were aware of the ray, but there was no response.

Less than two hours later, Rascal detected an unidentified object in the distance, directly in The HARM's navigational path. The object was tumbling end over end, uncontrolled. General Boxdale adjusted THE HARM's speed to intercept it. As we drew alongside, we realized it was an escape pod. Rascal confirmed it was from an earlier New Earth mission that had gone missing and was presumed lost.

We positioned THE HARM's robotic arms to grab the escape pod and pull it into the cargo bay. As the hatch hissed open, we discovered the bodies of two New Earth mission personnel, still in their uniforms with name tags - Captain Von Sloss and Lieutenant Nahema. According to Rascal's memory banks, their mission was The Galaxy Three, which had launched from New Africa five years ago and was presumed lost in a catastrophic explosion. By some miracle, they managed to launch the escape pod before the blast but found no way to return to New Earth.

We held a brief videotaped memorial service and solemnly released their remains into space. Attempts to contact MCC about the discovery were futile. This grim encounter reminded us of the inherent dangers of space missions. A few days later, as we exited Moonara's orbit, we released the escape pod into the void. It was a sobering start to our mission. General Boxdale, ever the stern leader, reminded us to stay focused on the journey ahead.

Days have turned into weeks, and we still haven't heard from New Earth. During our morning meetings, Rascal, our AI companion, tried to lift our spirits with its corny jokes. "Did you hear about the animal that got hit with a can of soda? Don't worry; it was a soft drink." Or "What's the easiest way to get straight A's? Use a ruler." Despite ourselves, we laughed – the jokes were so bad they were good.

Our mission, HARM, was now in full swing. Untethered from our seats, we reported to our assigned tasks. Our first destination was Planet C-1954, a distant world 973 light-years away. It would take us about six months to get there. We knew very little about this planet; minimal research had been conducted. On our return trip, we planned to investigate Planet A-1978. Our final stop before heading back to New Earth was Planet N-1990, a world with some known data, though it wasn't promising. Yet, we were determined to explore every possibility in our quest to save our starving, water-deficient home planet. As we settled into our routines, cruising through light years, a sense of boredom began to set in. But that was about to change dramatically.

Chapter 9.
The Surprise

Sergeant Z wakes up early every morning to make his security patrols. As usual, he traveled to the cargo bay, inspected it, and was about to leave when he heard a faint rattling noise. He stopped, listening closely. Nothing for a few seconds, and then the noise came again. He walked in the direction of the sound, unholstering the short WOL strapped to his side. The rattling grew louder as he approached. Banging on the metal container where the noise originated, he noted it was large enough to fit a medium-sized child or animal. The latch was not locked. Holding his WOL in one hand, he lifted the container top with the other. To his utter surprise, crouched in a near-fetal position, was a human. He commanded her to get up, and she complied. She was a female human, looking tired, exhausted, disheveled, afraid, and malnourished—a stowaway. Sergeant Z didn't recognize her, but she seemed vaguely familiar. He detained her, securing zip ties around her wrists. He asked only one question: "What is your name?" "My name is Lieutenant Jancedar," she replied. Sergeant Z immediately brought her to General Boxdale.

General Boxdale met privately with Lieutenant Jancedar, undoubtedly with a million questions on his mind. Later, I discovered that she had applied to be assigned to the HARM but was denied by MCC. General Boxdale told me that he found out later through an unofficial MCC source that a powerful MCC Board of Deciders member convinced the entire Board to deny her request; it was personal, not connected to the mission. Immediately, General Boxdale called a meeting of all crew members, and Lieutenant Jancedar was present. When The Ma'am saw her, she was shocked. Seeing her as a stowaway was different from knowing her as the Lieutenant who assisted her. But, being a compassionate person, she showed empathy towards Lieutenant Jancedar. General Boxdale briefed us on how Lieutenant Jancedar ended up on the mission. He had contacted MCC for further instructions and informed us that she would remain confined to her quarters until an official response was received.

Despite the unfortunate circumstances, the General expressed hope that MCC would permit Lieutenant

Jancedar to continue her specialized food research work. After recalculating the onboard resources—food, oxygen, and fuel—General Boxdale confirmed that the mission could proceed as planned without any disruptions. This was a relief for everyone. Most importantly, he revealed a startling discovery: she was a Pi-thar.

Chapter 10a.
The First Arrival

W e were approaching the halfway mark to Planet C-1954, a destination New Earth had never dared to explore. Deploying the mini-JWST, we observed an array of exoplanets in the distance orbiting around stars. The view was mesmerizing and fascinating! Suddenly, a bizarre phenomenon occurred. All of The HARM's instrumentation malfunctioned without any error codes or sounds. The spacecraft halted abruptly, engines dead. We were immobilized, enveloped in total darkness inside and outside the spacecraft. Only our voices pierced the eerie silence. Strangely, no oxygen circulated, yet we could breathe effortlessly. It felt like being trapped in mud, suspended in space and time. Fear gripped me like never before.

We grabbed our nuclear-energized flashlights, but after a few hours, they too failed. Gathering in the navigation department, Rascal tried to lighten the mood with jokes.

Despite his efforts, fear and uncertainty prevailed. For twelve agonizing hours, we waited, clueless about the cause of the phenomenon or how to escape it. The tension was palpable, and it was the most terrifying I had ever felt. Then, without warning, everything returned to normal, as if nothing had happened. The telemetry readings were unchanged, but we found ourselves several light years closer to Planet C-1954. To this day, there's no plausible explanation for what occurred. I never want to feel that vulnerable again. I can only imagine how General Boxdale must have felt.

Three months later, Planet C-1954 loomed on the horizon. Its light brownish hue was mesmerizing. As we approached, our anticipation grew. What would we find? What was the oxygen percentage? Would the soil support farming? What was gravity like? Were there foundational elements for water? These questions swirled in my mind. We descended into Planet C-1954's orbit, the final countdown to touchdown at the Landing Zone (LZ). "We are here!" Rascal shouted—the first stop on our HARM quest.

We suited up in our space gear and double-checked our instrumentation. General Boxdale granted me permission for a standard two-kilometer radius reconnaissance flight, the first-ever species to set foot on this planet. The hatch opened, and I took flight. Wow! What a view—peaks and valleys, sand and boulders. After the initial reconnaissance flight, I reported back to General Boxdale with my observations. He then authorized a ground patrol to further investigate potential food and water resources.

With all systems in order, General Boxdale gave permission for The Ma'am, Sergeant Z, Private Prissy, and Rascal to take the first research walk on Planet C-1954. I had briefed them on my observations from the initial reconnaissance flight. They put on their space gear, checked each other thoroughly, and, as the hatch opened, descended the steps onto the planet's surface. To their knowledge, no other species had ever set foot here.

Rascal, trying to lighten the mood, teased, "Be afraid, be very afraid," followed by his signature corny laugh. The rest of the team chuckled nervously, the reality of their mission sinking in. Stepping onto an alien planet was both eerie and exhilarating.

Sergeant Z led the way, his Long WOL weapon at the ready. According to their after-action report, they explored a one-kilometer radius around THE HARM. The Ma'am collected rock and soil samples along the way. The excursion lasted about two and a half hours. Back on the spacecraft, they began testing the samples.

Over the next three days, while the samples were analyzed, they noticed a yellowish light on the horizon, growing brighter and closer each day. On the fourth day, a ferocious windstorm hit, with the anemometer recording speeds of 160 kilometers per hour. They anchored the spacecraft as a precaution. The planet's topography was inhospitable, and gravity was about half of what it was on New Earth. There was no sign of life and no breathable air.

After the winds subsided, the crew gathered to hear The Ma'am's report on the soil and rock samples. She explained that she had used time-domain reflectometry (TDR), electrical resistivity tomography, frequency domain sensors, neutron probes, capacitance probes, and electrical resistivity tomography—all sensitive to the physical properties of water. Over the next two weeks, they gathered and tested samples from various locations, all with the same negative results. When her primary instrument, the Ground Penetrating Radar (GPR) also came up negative, she was certain that no potential water source existed on the planet. No water meant no potential food source. With this information, General Boxdale decided to start the journey back toward New Earth and move on to Planet A-1978, which was about halfway between their current location and New Earth.

Chapter 10b.
The Second Arrival

———◆O◆———

As we flew out of Planet C-1954's orbit, we were all disappointed by our failure to find a potential water source, especially The Ma'am. That evening, we gathered for an impromptu encouragement party for her. Everyone came except General Boxdale and, of course, Lieutenant Jancedar, who was confined to her quarters. Rascal sensed the mood and told jokes to lift our spirits, and the crew welcomed the distraction. Afterward, The Ma'am got permission from General Boxdale to visit Lieutenant Jancedar. The Lieutenant was glad to see The Ma'am, and the feeling was mutual. They had a long conversation about the findings on Planet C-1954 and looked forward to hopefully better results on HARM's next two scheduled research stops.

Back to the daily grind of on-board tasks, as the light years ticked away, the disappointment of Planet C-1954 became a distant memory. The crew looked ahead toward the promise of Planet A-1978. Then, an essential navigational instrument began to malfunction. Sergeant Waddles was called upon to repair it. After two days of diagnosing the problem, it turned out to be a faulty Radio Magnetic Indicator (RMI), which displays the spacecraft's heading with navigational bearing data. Sergeant Waddles repaired it, and we were all excited to continue our mission.

General Boxdale reported that he had still not heard from MCC regarding Lieutenant Jancedar, and she would remain confined to her quarters. The Ma'am was disappointed but understood the General's rationale. If every service member chose not to follow orders, chaos would ensue.

As we cruised toward Planet A-1978, there appeared to be no significant problems with our spacecraft or the crew. There were occasional family arguments over mundane things like food choices, lavatory duties, and laundry details, but no major issues. We spoke too soon. Through one of the large portholes, we saw a mirror image of our ship directly in front of us, facing us head-to-head through the mist of a light green smoke-like substance. It was surreal to see The HARM's reflection through the large porthole. Despite the odd sight, we had no trouble navigating, and all spacecraft functions were operating normally. For two days, we floated in this mist. Our onboard instruments tried to analyze the makeup of the matter but failed. On to Planet A-1978 we went, with a sense of mystery lingering in the air.

The crew did their best to shield Se-rye from any negative news. Occasionally, General Boxdale allowed Rascal to spend time with Se-rye, sharing age-appropriate jokes or assisting with her studies. Due to ongoing issues with Se-rye's online education and Lieutenant Jancedar being confined to quarters, the Lieutenant agreed to tutor Se-rye one-on-one. Private Prissy thought this was a fantastic idea. Over time, thanks to Se-rye, Lieutenant Jancedar and Private Prissy became good friends.

We soon encountered a microscopic meteor debris field—tiny, white pebbles floating around us. While they posed no navigation issues, they obscured our visibility. After a few days, the debris cleared, revealing a vast planet before us. To our amazement, it was Planet A-1978. It looked like a massive, sandpaper-textured sphere with dark spots marking immense craters. It was nearly twice the size of C-1954. Our navigation instruments indicated we were still several light-years away, yet there it was, right in front of us.

Suddenly, we were caught in its gravitational pull, accelerating at twice our normal speed. We found ourselves in A-1978's orbit, approaching at a dangerous 45-degree angle. General Boxdale and Sergeant Paw frantically tried to correct our course, but nothing worked. Just as General Boxdale was about to ask Rascal for recommendations, the gravitational pull stopped as abruptly as it had begun. Neither General Boxdale, Sergeant Paw, nor Rascal understood the cause, but they swiftly regained control of The HARM.

Slowly and methodically, we approached the designated landing area and gently set The HARM down at the LZ for Planet A-1978. The same crew that had researched Planet C-1954 was assigned to investigate. This time, our research would be more efficient, thanks to our previous experience. Rascal kept us laughing the whole way. The research and investigation of Planet A-1978 proceeded smoothly. After about a week, once all the data had been collected, The Ma'am called for a briefing. The results mirrored those of Planet C-1954: the potential water and food sources were harmful. As before, we held a gathering the evening before our scheduled departure, with Rascal lifting our spirits and pulling us out of our doldrums. As we prepared to leave the planet, Rascal voiced what the somber crew was thinking:

"We struck out again." But, with his usual optimism, he quickly added, "But we've got another opportunity coming up with Planet N-1990." With that cheerful thought, we all returned to our daily routines, ready to face the next challenge.

Chapter 10c.
The Third Arrival

According to the tellurometer, we were three-quarters of the way to Planet N-1990 when the temperature in The HARM spiked suddenly, causing several instruments to go offline.

"Look outside! Look outside!" Sergeant Waddles shouted, snapping us out of our focus. We turned to the portholes and gasped. A mesmerizing display of cloud-like formations had appeared, painted in brilliant hues of red, green, and purple.

"I've read about this phenomenon," Sergeant Waddles said, his voice steady despite the rising tension. "These are auroras, caused by magnetic explosions on the sun's surface. They're common side effects of solar flares with coronal mass ejections. These ejections emit X-rays and ultraviolet light, which interfere with electronics, satellites, and radio signals. They can also trigger solar radiation or geomagnetic storms." The gravity of the situation hit us as our radio telemetry instruments confirmed his words. "I strongly suggest we put on our Personal Protective Equipment (PPE) right now," Waddles continued. We scrambled to comply, the urgency in his voice leaving no room for hesitation.

Following Sergeant Waddle's advice, we quickly put on our PPE and deployed The HARM's sun shields. We kept our gear on for several days, only removing part of it to eat. We were about three-quarters of the way back to New Earth with nothing significant to report. Just a few light-years away from our final mission stop, Planet N-1990, the stakes were high. Anxiety levels spiked, and our behavior toward each other became increasingly tense. General Boxdale, sensing the mounting stress, called a crew meeting to calm us down. Rascal delivered a surprisingly heartfelt speech that lifted our spirits.

As we approached N-1990, our navigation was smooth. The planet, smaller than those we had previously visited, loomed dark and foreboding. After nearly nine months on this mission, we all hoped our research would yield positive results this time. On General Boxdale's order, we began our descent. The planet had no distinct features, appearing ominously dark. Unlike the previous planets, we executed a night landing in a small crater. We had to wait two days for daylight before we could disembark and start our research.

The research team, again consisting of The Ma'am, Sergeant Z, Private Prissy, and Rascal, expanded their initial radius to three kilometers. We collected soil and rock samples from five locations instead of three. With the samples in hand, The Ma'am and Private Prissy began their analysis. The increased number of samples meant a longer wait for the results. Finally, General Boxdale called for a meeting to discuss the findings. We were all on edge, eagerly awaiting The Ma'am's report.

The first thing out of The Ma'am's mouth was, "I have no good news to report." Our hearts collectively sank. She explained that every test had come up negative for potential water or food sources. The room was so silent that you could hear a pin drop. Our expressions mirrored the grief of losing a loved one. Rascal, sensing the heaviness of the moment, stayed quiet. Then, with a firm voice, General Boxdale said, "We have work to do, folks. Let's prepare for our final leg home." With that, the crew dispersed to their usual duty stations. There were no celebrations and no positive thoughts in the following days.

Everyone carried on with their tasks, each of us haunted by the thought that we had failed our mission.

Days later, at the end of our daily morning meeting, Rascal decided to lighten the mood with a few jokes. I remember some of them. "Where should you work if you want to tell anyone their fortune? The bank. Why do they serve snails at fancy restaurants? Because their customers don't like fast food. And what kind of books take the longest to read? Yearbooks." Rascal waited a few seconds after each question, then excitedly shouted the punchline. As corny as the jokes were, they made us laugh. This small gesture lifted our collective spirits, bringing a much-needed dose of positivity.

Chapter 11.
Homeward Bound, Maybe

A somber, almost melancholy mood swept over the crew as we caught the sun's orbit and began our final leg back to New Earth. Even Se-rye's normally cheerful disposition had faded. We were about five days away from New Earth and two days from our nearby home planet, Moonara, which we would pass along the way. Moonara had been researched and investigated countless times over the decades, but no valuable resources had ever been found.

Rascal tried to cheer us up, but his efforts fell flat. I couldn't imagine a worse outcome, but the General reminded us that we had traveled almost two and a half million kilometers and had successfully deployed a mini-JWST. He said, "It has acquired data that will be extremely useful to MCC. Once analyzed, some of its deep-field images will allow us to see and study thousands of distant galaxies. This data will also provide invaluable information for our planet's survival. For you young folks, the JWST, or the - Webb- as we called it, was initially launched in the early part of this century after decades of research, mistakes made, and billions of dollars spent. It was state-of-the-art technology then and remains the gold standard for space exploration today. It is the reason we can undertake this mission now." I nodded my head in agreement. The General was in his element now, talking about space, and Private Prissy was listening intently. The General continued, "Life is out there somewhere. Whether it's in The Pillars of Creation, just 6,500 light-years away, the Phantom Galaxy, 32 million light-years away, at Stephan's Quintet 290 million light-years away, or even at the Cartwheel Galaxy 500 million light-years away. Life is out there." He caught himself and said, "Well, children, class is over for recess," as he began laughing out loud. We all started laughing with him.

We began to plan the things we would do upon our return. We would probably be reassigned to other duty locations. I was looking forward to casual flights to visit family and friends. Even Saba'ta's folks seemed appealing at this point. It was the morning we were to sling around Planet Moonara. We were all making final preparations. General Boxdale and Sergeant Paw were busy making navigational instrument checks; Rascal was at his usual station close to General Boxdale; Sergeant Z was making physical security checks around The HARM and checking on Lieutenant Jancedar; Sergeant Waddles was taking inventory of the munitions on hand; The Ma'am and Private Prissy were organizing all the soil and rock samples retrieved to be turned over to MCC for further analysis; Se-rye was completing her online classes in her quarters; Lieutenant Jancedar was still confined to her quarters; and I was in my quarters eating breakfast and reflecting on our mission travels. Whew! It's been an adventure, I thought, but this mission is almost over.

Chapter 12.
And Then

As we embarked on the final leg of our mission back to New Earth, disappointment hung over us like a dark cloud. Three planets, three failures—no food or water sources discovered. Yet, operationally, the HARM had gone according to plan for nearly the whole time, barring the unexplained events. But that was about to change drastically. Suddenly, bursts of multicolored designs flashed through The HARM's portholes, reminiscent of old Independence Day celebrations. But this was no video or recording—we were in the middle of the spectacle. These radiant displays enveloped us, casting a surreal glow inside the spacecraft. Despite the dazzling show, The HARM remained unaffected. For the better part of the day, we traveled through this cosmic fireworks display. It was unexpected and exhilarating. Rascal started singing the Star-Spangled Banner, and we all joined in, my eyes welling up with tears.

Two days blurred by as we hurtled through space towards home. Just as we approached Planet Moonara for the sling maneuver back to New Earth, an asteroid storm erupted around us, battering The HARM mercilessly. Moonara's magnetic pull gripped us, dragging The HARM sideways and out of control. General Boxdale and Sergeant Paw fought desperately to regain control, but it was futile. In the chaos, debris inside the spacecraft struck General Boxdale in the head, knocking him unconscious.

Following protocol, Rascal sent a distress message to MCC, unsure if it would reach New Earth, and immediately took control of The HARM, with Sergeant Paw assisting. General Boxdale regained consciousness, but his vision was blurred, leaving Rascal at the helm. Moments later, we plunged into Moonara's orbit. Rascal deployed the heat shields. We were hurling sideways into Moonara's atmosphere, pounded by asteroid debris at 30,000 kilometers per hour, the heat soaring to 5,000 degrees (2,760 Celsius). Five agonizing minutes felt like an eternity.

We had no choice but to land on Planet Moonara. The bad news kept piling up. During a wellness check, we discovered that The Ma'am was sick again. Her undetected pre-existing condition was worsened by our rough entry toward

Moonara. The crew was deeply concerned. Sergeant Paw noticed that Rascal was acting erratically and providing inaccurate instrument readings. The asteroid storm's magnetic signature had interfered with his nano computer circuits. Unable to repair it until after The HARM touched down, Sergeant Paw took Rascal offline and assumed sole responsibility for piloting and navigation. Se-rye, fearful for the first time, clung to Private Prissy, not wanting her to leave her side.

We were now on an inevitable course to land on Moonara. Sergeant Paw desperately tried to regain control of The HARM. He managed to restart two of the four rocket engines, enabling some guidance systems. He operationalized the thrusters and drag flaps, crucial for avoiding a catastrophic crash landing. The HARM shook violently as we entered Moonara's atmosphere, and so did we. These were tense moments, but Sergeant Paw rose to the occasion. Fully aware of the high stakes, he landed The HARM on Moonara's yet-to-be-discovered dark side with remarkable professionalism. We skipped across the planet's surface like a stone skimming across a pond on New Earth before coming to a complete stop. We sat in stunned silence, staring at each other. Then Sergeant Paw, now jokingly, roared, "WE'RE HERE!"

We had landed in a small shallow crater on Moonara's dark side, about 370,000 kilometers from New Earth—a three-day journey. My years of flight study told me we were at the South Pole, a place of eternal darkness, where surface temperatures can reach -250 degrees Fahrenheit (-156.6 Celsius), and where some large craters have never seen sunlight. With General Boxdale still temporarily impaired, I was the next highest-ranking officer. I ordered the crew to their respective duty stations to assess the situation and reconvene in the navigation compartment at 1700 hours. During our meeting, I shared that we faced a grim reality; the journey back to New Earth was impossible due to severe damage to The HARM. To make matters worse, most of our food and water supplies had been destroyed during our chaotic entry and landing on Moonara. As if things couldn't get worse, Sergeant Paw reported that Rascal had confided in him a few days earlier that Lieutenant Jancedar was a Pi-Thar and that she was not to be trusted. She had manipulated her DNA results to secure a position on our mission. Her goal was to uncover and steal any breakthrough food research results we discovered for her own ambition. This was also why she had stowed away on The HARM.

I ordered the crew to get a good night's sleep and announced that we would reconvene the following morning at 0700 hours. At 0530 hours the next day, I was already awake. I gazed out my port side window at the light pink landscape outside. After a brief prayer, I exercised, showered, brushed my wings, ate breakfast, and left my quarters for the meeting.

Just before the meeting, General Boxdale asked me to lead it. He mentioned that while his blurriness had almost disappeared, he was still not feeling one hundred percent. So, at 0700 hours sharp, I started the meeting. Our first task was to inspect the damage to The HARM. However, Sergeant Paw requested a short delay to repair Rascal, believing his assistance would be invaluable under the current circumstances. I agreed and scheduled the inspection for later in the day.

After completing the repairs, Sergeant Paw informed me that Rascal was ready. With his usual humor, Rascal quipped, "I'm glad to be back among the living and of sound mind," followed by his signature corny, infectious laugh. Given the unexpected situation, only Sergeant Z, Sergeant Paw, and Rascal would participate in the inspection. At 1400 hours, the walkabout team suited up in their space gear and ventured outside. Daylight filtered through the thin atmosphere, their helmet lights illuminating the path ahead. As they traversed the hull of The HARM, the extent of the spacecraft's damage became starkly evident. They meticulously documented their findings with video recordings, crucial for the crew's assessment upon their return.

At the end of the briefing with the crew regarding the damage to The HARM, I consulted with General Boxdale and reported that since we would be on Planet Moonara for a while, we would set up a base camp. This would be similar to what we would have done if we had found food or water sources on any of the three planets we visited on this mission. The setup would be straightforward, as everything had been prefabricated. We were to begin installing the base camp the following day. The name had already been chosen before we departed on the mission— it would be called "Camp Salute."

Early the next day, around 0300 hours, I was informed that Se-rye had woken her aunt, Private Prissy, complaining that she couldn't sleep because of a light shining in her eyes. When Private Prissy investigated, she saw through the window what looked like a one-color aurora sky, similar to those once seen on New Earth. This aurora was a light pastel pink, hovering just above the planet's mountain ranges. Everything was bathed in this light pink hue. Private Prissy ran to wake me to see if I knew about it. I told her that I did. I slid back the window covering, confirming what she saw, and told her we would wait until our 0700 meeting to discuss it further with the crew.

At the beginning of the meeting with the crew, all anyone could talk about was the pink light. A thousand questions ran through our minds: Where did it come from? Who put it there? How long would it last? Was it dangerous? We pondered endlessly. Due to the uncertainty, I volunteered to make an initial reconnaissance flight. Based on my findings, we would then discuss the next steps. I put on my space helmet (all I needed because of my DNA), stepped into the hatch doorway, and began my flight. It was extremely cold but manageable for my DNA.

I must say, the scenery was beautiful, even in that pastel pink light. As I flew, I noticed one of the mountain ranges was shaded in light and dark purple. I thought to myself, I need to investigate that mountain further. Upon closer inspection, I discovered the light was coming from an incandescent ground-cover plant that emitted a glow. This plant clung to the mountain's outer rocks, with another light source emanating from within the mountain.

After a flight covering about a five-kilometer radius, I returned to The HARM. I briefed the crew on what I had observed. There appeared to be no life forms on the planet, consistent with the research conducted on New Earth over the decades. With that in mind, I directed Sergeant Z, Sergeant Waddles, Sergeant Paw, and Rascal to investigate the five-kilometer radius I had just explored, especially the area where I observed the purplish mountain phenomenon. They were to move out the following day.

Chapter 13.
We Are Not Alone

It had been nearly a week since we landed. General Boxdale had fully recovered and resumed command. As our morning meeting ended, Sergeant Z slung his long gun WOL over his shoulder, ready to depart. Meanwhile, Sergeant Waddles packed his backpack with WOL paks and short-range explosives, securing a small WOL under his wing. Rascal, always the joker, quipped as they prepared to depart, "You guys better protect me, okay?" before bursting into laughter. I took to the skies as the overhead scout.

Sergeant Z led the ground team while I circled above. We were approximately two kilometers from the purplish mountain range I had discovered the day before. Maintaining open transmitter contact, I listened intently as Sergeant Z murmured, "Something at 1300," pointing his WOL in that direction. Using my keen long-range vision, I circled once before perching high on a nearby rock, keeping watch over the coordinates to avoid exposing Sergeant Z and his crew.

The ground team advanced cautiously toward the sporadic rattling noise, taking cover behind occasional boulders. They huddled behind a large rock as a four-foot-tall, one-eyed brownish being appeared just twenty-five meters away. It moved hesitantly, sensing their presence. I alerted Sergeant Z, who acknowledged silently. The being froze in place, seemingly afraid, while our crew readied their WOLs behind cover. Later, Sergeant Z confided in me that they too felt a sense of unease.

Both sides stood at a tense standstill, each contemplating their next move. I gave Sergeant Z the authority to act at his discretion. Moments later, he rose swiftly and fired two short bursts from his long WOL, the distinct sizzle echoing through the air. The unknown being erupted into uncontrollable laughter, collapsing to the ground. With precision, Sergeant Z and Rascal secured the being in a breathable bag, while Sergeant Paw stood guard with his short WOL. I swooped down, grasped the bag with my claws, and swiftly returned it to The HARM. The ground crew followed suit, moving swiftly in our wake.

I relayed to The HARM that I was en route with our captive, ensuring preparations were made for secure containment upon arrival. By the time we returned, the being was safely confined, and the ground crew soon rejoined us. After briefing General Boxdale, he convened a meeting with the entire crew.

In the navigation compartment, we exchanged incredulous looks, stunned by the discovery of life on Planet Moonara, let alone such a peculiar form as the one we had captured. Countless questions raced through our minds, pondering the implications of this unprecedented encounter. General Boxdale outlined two immediate objectives: administering the antidote for the WOL to the being and dispatching a reconnaissance team for further investigation. He reasoned that if one of these beings existed, others would likely be present. As the meeting concluded, Rascal quipped, "So you guys are the Moonara 7," punctuating his statement with his characteristic laugh. Amused, we joined in, and the moniker stuck inexplicably, defining us as The Moonara 7 from that moment forward.

The Ma'am was still recovering, but well enough to administer the antidote. For security purposes, Sergeant Z accompanied her to the being's confinement area. After she administered the antidote, they both departed. Meanwhile, General Boxdale continued his attempts to contact MCC to update it regarding the situation. Opting not to terminate the being, the General prioritized gathering as much information as possible. Two days passed as they strategized their approach.

On the third morning, Rascal noticed on the video monitor that the being was awake and moving around in its confinement area. Alerting General Boxdale, they, along with The Ma'am and Rascal, approached the area to communicate with it. As they entered, the being recoiled against the wall, clearly afraid. I observed everything on the video monitor.

General Boxdale questioned the being about its identity, the presence of others like it, and its ability to understand. However, it remained unresponsive. As they were leaving, Rascal adjusted a circuit, emitting a pulse-like beep. Surprisingly, the being responded with a similar sound from its hands and mouth, moving them in a synchronized manner. The team paused. General Boxdale asked Rascal if he comprehended the being's response, but Rascal shook his head affirming the negative. They exited the room, leaving General Boxdale to instruct Rascal to return alone later for further attempts to communicate.

Day after day, Rascal spent hours alone with the being, yet communication remained elusive. Meanwhile, Sergeant Z, alongside Sergeant Waddles and Sergeant Paw, embarked on investigative walkabouts in the sector of the planet where they were forced to land. Their mission is to discover more beings like the one captured, explore the mysterious purplish mountain distinct from the rest, and learn more about the source of the pink light and purplish light.

The following day, as on previous days, Rascal returned to the area where the being was being held. We had left food and water, but they remained untouched. Watching live on the video monitors, we observed Rascal stretching out his hand for the first time to gauge the being's reaction. There was none. As Rascal moved closer, the being retreated as it had before.

Then, something extraordinary happened. Rascal emitted an audible high-pitched sound, adjusting his electronic computer nanocircuits. No words, just a sound. To our amazement, the being responded with a sound of its own. It raised its arms straight out in front of it, horizontally at chest level, and made a single sound, "E-yak" (pronounced

E-y-ak). This was a breakthrough! We were witnessing history in the making.

With this initial success, Rascal utilized its extensive sound memory bank to continue attempts at communication. We moved Rascal's docking station next to the being's confinement area for easier access. Inspired by the being's first word, we named the species "Enac."

Day by day, as Rascal aligned its electronic nanocircuit frequency with the Enac, communication became clearer and more rapid. Weeks of intensive exchanges between Rascal and the Enac yielded valuable insights into the Enacs' nature and the region of Planet Moonara they inhabited. Through Rascal's communication with the Enac and its translation to the rest of the crew, we learned that the Enac species live exclusively underground in caves on Planet Moonara's dark side. They only emerge occasionally to gather sharp detached rocks used for cutting. Hundreds of years ago, the Enacs (whom we called Enacamytes) discovered a light-producing plant that thrives underground without any cultivation. This plant grows in the very caves where they reside. They have developed a method to harness this light when they venture above ground.

To explain it in familiar terms, imagine a diffuse reflection: a beam of light hits a rough object and scatters in all directions. Over decades of trial and error, the Enacamytes perfected this process, allowing them to enjoy light above ground, although limited in duration and range. The concave-shaped plant emits a soft pink glow, and the Enacs string several of them together, directing the light upward. They refer to this phenomenon as the "Upper Dome" or "Bright Dome." When the light dims, it signals that the plants are dying and need replacement.

While progress was being made in communicating with the Enac, our onboard food supply dwindled to less than two weeks. General Boxdale was deeply concerned, and no immediate solution was in sight. Rascal had gained the Enacs trust, and while the antidote it received was successful, the Enac began to weaken. It could not eat our food and could only digest our water, leading to severe malnutrition. Recognizing the urgency, General Boxdale authorized a mission to return the Enac to its habitat underground near the mountain range where we found it (We named it Mt. Moonara).

Chapter 14.
Returning It Home

It was a sleepless night for all of us, filled with a mix of excitement and anticipation about what we might discover when returning the Enac to its home. At the same time, a sense of fear loomed over us about what lay ahead. The day of the journey had finally arrived. General Boxdale had stressed that this was a security mission, restricted to security personnel and Rascal. This meant that Rascal would be accompanied by Sergeant Z, Sergeant Waddles, and Sergeant Paw (Rascal's handler). My role was to provide overhead reconnaissance.

The team marched toward Mt. Moonara, the Enac leading the way with Rascal close behind. After several hours, we arrived at what appeared to be a small, hollowed-out opening about a hundred meters from the mountain's base. The Enac entered the cave, followed cautiously by our ground crew, weapons on alert. Sergeant Z later recounted the discovery of an elaborate underground system of wide tunnels that seemed ancient. The tunnels were lit, with pink plants lining the walls as a light source, just as the Enac had described. These tunnels led to a vast opening where the ceiling soared thirty to forty meters high. The Enac instructed Rascal to have us stop and wait in the large opening. The creature then ventured further into another tunnel. We stood there, anxiously waiting, each second stretching into what felt like an eternity. In reality, it was only about five to ten minutes.

THE ENAC SUPREME

From the same tunnel the Enac had entered, another figure emerged, taller and more robust. The two Enacs approached and stood silently before us, their stillness unsettling. After a tense moment, the Enac with us began to communicate with Rascal, introducing the newcomer as its leader. Rascal conveyed that the leader's name was "The Enac Supreme" and that it expressed gratitude for our care of its young grandson, "Bebe." This was the first time we learned the name of the Enac we had tended to. The Enac Supreme explained that their species was peaceful and deeply indebted to us for protecting Bebe, who shouldn't have been above ground alone. It appeared that Bebe was a teenager.

We were stunned, a mix of amazement, curiosity, and disbelief rendering us momentarily speechless. Sergeant Z, our mission leader, broke the silence, instructing Rascal to relay our appreciation and assure them of our peaceful intentions as well. The Enac Supreme then gestured towards one of the tunnels, and suddenly, a large host of Enacs flooded the room. The sight was both thrilling and terrifying. Sergeant Paw requested Rascal to inform Enac Supreme that our leader, General Boxdale, wished to meet with it at the earliest opportunity. Enac Supreme graciously agreed. Enac Bebe led the ground crew back through the tunnels, bidding us farewell at the entrance we had initially used. I felt a wave of relief seeing the ground crew safe, reassured by how well things had turned out. As we made our way back to The HARM, we exchanged excited conversations about our experience. The consensus was clear: this species was indeed peaceful. We reported everything to General Boxdale, who was eager to meet with Enac Supreme and further our interspecies relationship.

Chapter 15.
Eureka!

eneral Boxdale, Sergeant Z, Rascal, and I set out to meet with The Enac Supreme early the following morning. Upon arrival at the designated opening, we were greeted by two Enacamytes, who stood about two meters apart, first exchanging glances before focusing on us. This time, I was part of the ground crew, ready to observe and assist.

As we approached, The Enac Supreme stood waiting, exuding an aura of authority and intensity that seemed to penetrate one's very soul with a single, unwavering eye. Despite the simplicity of its appearance, The Enac Supreme commanded respect, a light purple sash elegantly draped across its body from shoulder to waist. Later, I learned that The Enac Supreme had inherited its position from its father and had been leading the Enacamytes for over forty years. Its word was absolute.

Enac Bebe, the translator, was also present to facilitate communication with Rascal. The Enac Supreme raised its arms horizontally, at chest height, and uttered sounds that Enac Bebe translated as, "We are glad you are here." General Boxdale responded through Rascal, expressing his pleasure in meeting The Enac Supreme. At this point, The Enac Supreme introduced its second-in-command, Enac Grand. Though formal and authoritative, Enac Grand lacked the warmth of The Enac Supreme. The introductions completed, General Boxdale and The Enac Supreme, with Enac Bebe and Rascal tagging along as translators, moved to a smaller, more secluded area for a private discussion that lasted several hours. During this critical conversation, The Enac Supreme disclosed information that had the potential to alter the course of history for New Earth. The gravity of the news left General Boxdale visibly shaken, as we realized the implications of what was revealed.

The Enac Supreme revealed that its species' food source might be suitable for us and, if so, would be willing to share as much as New Earth needed. Upon hearing this, I thought, "We've traveled hundreds of lightyears from home over many months, and now we might find a permanent food source just three days away. Incredible!" General Boxdale asked and received permission from The Enac Supreme to investigate the food resource possibilities on Mt. Moonara. The Enac Supreme also appointed Enac Grand to guide us up the mountain on our expedition. General Boxdale informed The Enac Supreme that we would establish our base camp closer to Mt. Moonara for easier access. The Enac Supreme agreed.

At our regular 0700 hours meeting the next day, General Boxdale briefed the entire crew on his meeting with The Enac Supreme. We began planning the food research expedition to Mt. Moonara. As you can imagine we were all thrilled, especially The Ma'am! Our first task was to set up base camp. This was an all-hands-on-deck task. Only Rascal was to remain on The HARM, managing its systems, along with The Ma'am due to her illness. Lieutenant Jancedar was still confined to her quarters. We selected a site for Camp Salute and built it in three days. We returned to The HARM exhausted. After recuperating, we were ready to deploy for the food source expedition.

The Ma'am was still not well enough to join the mission. Despite Lieutenant Jancedar being revealed as a Pi-Thar, General Boxdale decided to include her in the research mission to Mt. Moonara because of her expertise in food and water research. Private Prissy lacked experience in conducting food research. However, he gave Sergeant Z and Private Prissy specific orders to observe her closely.

We began our journey to our new home near the base of Mt. Moonara, specifically Camp Salute. A small rover carried our essentials, but the rugged terrain and 50% gravity slowed our progress. Our bulky space gear made the environment a formidable and dangerous adversary. Finally, we reached Camp Salute, unpacked, and settled in for the night. I ventured outside briefly, gazing across the base camp towards the spiked peaks of Mt. Moonara. The mountain, often referred to simply as "Moonara," loomed majestically under the whistling solar winds. Its high, white peaks resembled snow, but I would later discover they were composed of sodium deposits.

As dawn broke, it was time for our food expedition. Sergeant Z, Sergeant Paw, Lieutenant Jancedar, Private Prissy, Rascal, and I (Colonel Swift) set out to meet Enac Grand. This was Lieutenant Jancedar's first expedition, and her amazement was palpable. Upon meeting Enac Grand and conducting introductions, we turned our gaze to Moonara. At approximately 10,000 meters tall, it was nearly a third the height of Mt. Everest on New Earth. The reduced gravity promised to shorten the climb to the peak, but it would still take several days.

General Boxdale had instructed me to conduct a reconnaissance flight to Moonara's peak before the main ascent to understand the challenges ahead. While Enac Grand and our crew began the climb, I took to the skies in a swift reconnaissance flight. My aerial survey would be quicker, allowing me to rejoin the mission crew as they advanced up the mountain. As I soared alongside Moonara, the solar winds began to intensify, making it a bit trickier to maintain a steady flight path. Yet, navigating through the skies wasn't too troublesome. At my rapid pace, I reached the peak of Moonara in less than a day, though I was utterly exhausted. I found a comfortable rock ledge to rest for the night. After a rejuvenating sleep, I set out to explore the peak. The first thing that struck me was that the peak was a vast crater. I resisted the urge to descend into it, choosing instead to wait for the rest of the crew. I then embarked on the return flight to rejoin my crewmates and Enac Grand.

Upon reuniting with the crew and Enac Grand, I reported my findings from Moonara's peak. The crew was buzzing with excitement, but Enac Grand remained silent. We couldn't determine if Enac Grand was naturally reserved or if there was something else at play. We camped on Moonara's ledges for three nights. On the fourth morning, we estimated we would reach the peak by the end of the day. As we ascended, a sudden, fierce solar wind struck us. Enac Grand led us. Following his lead, we found shelter in a small indentation on the mountain. It wasn't a cave, but it was spacious enough to shield us from the wind. Whether the Enacamytes had carved this space, or it was a natural formation, we didn't know. Regardless, it provided us protection.

The wind gusted at speeds up to one hundred kilometers per hour, howling for hours on end. We waited so long that we eventually fell asleep. Morning arrived, and the wind had calmed. We emerged from our shelter and continued our ascent; it was day five. We could now see the white peak of Moonara; we were almost there. With one final push, we reached the peak at approximately 1530 hours. Our crew was exhausted, but Enac Grand appeared unaffected, perhaps a testament to its DNA, having adapted to the planet's environment. I decided we would camp overnight in a small plateau-like space just below the peak.

It was the morning of the sixth day, and our anticipation to explore Mt. Moonara's peak was palpable. The crew gathered for breakfast, and I couldn't help but notice Enac Grand consuming a small, purplish, plant-like substance. As we trekked towards the peak, a realization struck me—it was my birthday, September 27th. Private Prissy cheerfully reminded me that it was also Se-rye's birthday. She mentioned that The Ma'am had promised to celebrate with her niece back at Camp Salute and would celebrate with her again upon our return.

Following Enac Grand, we ventured onto a well-worn path along the ridge of the peak. The pink light of dawn illuminated the crater I had glimpsed days earlier. We froze in our tracks, stunned by what lay before us. Inside the crater, a miraculous sight awaited: a small, purplish, vegetable-like substance growing abundantly along the inner walls of the ridge. Enac Grand grabbed a piece, broke it off, and ate it without hesitation.

However, we were uncertain if it was safe for us. Sergeant Paw turned to Rascal, our resilient companion immune to all, to test and analyze the plant. Rascal methodically broke off a piece and consumed it. After a few tense minutes, Rascal shared the analysis results. "It contains all seven essential elements to sustain both human and animal life—carbohydrates, protein, fat, fiber, vitamins, minerals, and water. Additionally, it has minerals that could significantly enhance our health," Rascal reported. We were beyond excited! I tried to communicate our news to General Boxdale at Camp Salute, but there was too much interference due to our altitude. For our purposes, we would later name this food source "Dark Life Vegetation." But for now, as we calmed down a little, we continued to follow Enac Grand down the ridgeline of the crater.

We had not gone more than twenty-five meters when we saw ahead what appeared to be something solid and light purple stuck to the ridgeline wall. It couldn't be what my mind was thinking. No, no, no, I said to myself. As we approached, Sergeant Paw directed Rascal to touch it and analyze what it was made of. Rascal did, and the results came back as having the properties of water and good old H2O. He then broke off a piece and ate it, confirming its initial results. We called it the "Purple Freeze." Lieutenant Jancedar and Private Prissy also tested it and came up with the same field results as Rascal. Unbelievable is a gross understatement of how we were feeling. Two life-sustaining finds in one day, in the same place.

After a few more hours lingering in the crater, we gathered samples of the "dark life vegetation" and what we dubbed the "purple freeze" before beginning our descent back to Camp Salute. We chose not to contact base camp about our discovery, wanting to deliver the good news in person. The return trip promised to be much shorter than our initial trek up the mountain. Each night, as we rested, our conversations revolved solely around the marvels we had encountered and the potential salvation they represented for New Earth. The air buzzed with a mixture of excitement and hope.

Upon our arrival at Camp Salute, we were greeted with eager anticipation. General Boxdale, The Ma'am, and Sergeant Waddles listened intently as we recounted our findings. General Boxdale, his voice tinged with rare optimism, spoke of the implications for the animal and human species on New Earth. "This discovery," he said, "could be the second chance we desperately needed—a chance to rectify past mistakes and ensure the long-term survival of New Earth."

MCC continued to be left in the dark about our status, unsure if we had landed or perished somewhere in the galaxies. General Boxdale emphasized two urgent objectives: reconnect our comms to report our breakthrough to MCC and repair The HARM for our journey home. Meanwhile, The Ma'am and Private Prissy were engrossed in analyzing the dark life vegetation and the purple freeze. Their findings confirmed our initial conclusions, further cementing the significance of our discovery.

Chapter 16.
Help Wanted

In the following days, we sought out The Enac Supreme, inquiring if it possessed any technology capable of aiding us in the repair of our spacecraft. The Enac Supreme admitted that it did not have the technology, but it mentioned its grandson, Enac Bebe, who had a unique ability to see through anything broken and reverse-engineer it to its original state. However, there was uncertainty if this gift would work on our spacecraft. Despite this, The Enac Supreme expressed a willingness to have Enac Bebe try, especially with Rascal's assistance.

Weeks passed, and as our onboard food supply dwindled, we resorted to consuming the Dark Life vegetation. Fortunately, our water supply remained intact. To our surprise, a mere six-ounce portion of the Dark Life vegetation kept us energized throughout the day. Although the long-term effects were unknown, it was the perfect solution for our immediate needs.

Enac Bebe and Rascal formed an unlikely but effective partnership, meticulously working to repair The HARM. The Enacs possessed natural materials far superior to our own, significantly aiding in the repair process. Despite a few of Rascal's circuits remaining unrestored, Sergeant Paw remained confident that we had the necessary resources to fix The HARM.

As Enac Bebe and Rascal worked closely together over time, it confided in Rascal that there was unrest among the Enacs. Enac Grand was opposed to The Enac Supreme granting us access to the Dark Life vegetation and the purple freeze. Despite the vast quantities of these resources, sufficient to last thousands of years across multiple planets, Enac Grand was unwilling to share with "outsiders." However, Enac Bebe assured us that its grandfather's word was law, and there was nothing Enac Grand could do to oppose it. Though this revelation was unsettling, it left us feeling cautiously optimistic about our situation.

Chapter 17.
The Food Fight

———◆◆◆———

Today, we began testing the systems on The Harm. Enac Bebe and Rascal had worked tirelessly for weeks on the spacecraft's systems and exterior hardware. We were about ninety percent complete with all repairs. So far, everything was a green light, but the real test would come in a couple of days when we would test-fire our rocket boosters and repair the thrusters. In the meantime, we learned from Enac Bebe that the disagreement between its grandfather, Enac Supreme, and Enac Grand had escalated. We didn't realize the extent of the conflict until much later.

It was make-or-break time as we fired up the rocket boosters and thrusters. Testing was successful, though we needed to tweak the thrusters slightly—a couple of hours of work. Planet Moonara's rotational sling window was approaching in a few days, and we were all busy preparing to launch toward New Earth.

The mission's crew was about to retire for the evening when Enac Bebe burst into Camp Salute in a panic. It said that Enac Grand, along with a few loyal followers, had kidnapped its grandfather, The Enac Supreme, and taken him up Mt. Moonara. Being a peaceful species, Enac Bebe didn't know what to do, so it came to us for help. General Boxdale immediately consulted with the crew and decided we had to rescue The Enac Supreme, especially since he had been so helpful and accommodating to us. Though we didn't want to get involved in an interplanetary incident, we couldn't stand by and do nothing. This required an all-hands-on-deck response. Only Rascal and Lieutenant Jancedar would remain at Camp Salute. Sergeant Paw had learned enough of the Enacs' language to communicate generally. Sergeant Z issued WOLs to everyone, including The Ma'am. Despite our varied military specialties, we are all soldiers now.

As we put on our specialized body armor and space gear, the crew followed Enac Bebe towards Mt. Moonara. At our usual meeting place, we were met by numerous Enacs, their faces etched with fear. They pointed frantically toward the peak of Mt. Moonara. General Boxdale gathered the crew and reminded us of the gravity of our mission; the fate of Planet New Earth hung in the balance.

My task was to fly ahead on a reconnaissance mission and gather intelligence regarding the situation. The old veteran, General Boxdale, delivered an inspiring speech, igniting our determination to confront the enemy head-on. He said, "We have trained our whole careers for times like these, and I am confident that with grit, determination, and an eye toward the future of New Earth, we shall prevail."

As I soared on my reconnaissance flight, the rest of the crew began their ascent. We left Enac Bebe with the other Enacs, ensuring their safety. With resolute purpose, we climbed Moonara, each step taken with cautious determination. By the end of day one, I rejoined the crew, reporting no sightings of any Enacamytes. Near the end of day two, halfway up the mountain, we spotted several Enacamytes hiding behind scattered rocks. Instantly, we took cover, wary of their intentions. Because of their peaceful nature, General Boxdale opted for a diplomatic approach, though our WOLs remained at the ready.

We had previously learned that the Enacamytes' only weapon was a hand-delivered halter device, designed to freeze targets temporarily. General Boxdale instructed Sergeant Paw to call out to the Enacamytes, conveying our desire for a peaceful resolution. We assured them we sought only to locate and bring home The Enac Supreme. We urged them to step out from behind the rocks if they wished to avoid conflict.

Minutes passed without movement. We repeated the message, and slowly, the Enacamytes emerged. Relief washed over me, though neither Enac Grand nor The Enac Supreme was among them. We asked if they knew where Enac Grand had taken The Enac Supreme. One Enacamyte revealed that Enac Grand had taken The Enac Supreme to the mountain's peak. We bound the Enacamytes we had encountered on the mountain, preparing to transport them back as we pressed onward up Moonara. Finally reaching the peak, we scanned the horizon but found no sign of Enac Grand or The Enac Supreme. Suddenly, from a small opening, Enac Grand emerged, arms raised and sprayed the halter device in a wide arc as we descended along the ridgeline into the crater. A slimy green, gel-like substance oozed from its mouth—later dubbed "sliyme." Most of it was missing, but Sergeant Waddles took a direct hit, paralyzing his leg.

Reacting swiftly, Sergeant Z returned fire, striking Enac Grand squarely in the center mask. The Enacamyte collapsed, uncontrollable laughter echoing as it fell.

General Boxdale and Sergeant Z secured our captive while The Ma'am administered a swift antidote to Sergeant Waddles. Ordered by General Boxdale, I airlifted Enac Grand back to Camp Salute, leaving the team to continue the hunt for The Enac Supreme. Hours passed as we scoured the area, but The Enac Supreme had still not been found.

About half a kilometer down inside the crater Private Prissy heard a faint sound. Due to Moonara's magnetic interference, she couldn't contact another crewmate. Undeterred, she followed the sound, which grew louder and louder until she reached its source, though she saw nothing. Using the barrel of her long WOL, she poked the side of the mountain in several places. Suddenly, a small entry point opened, just large enough for an object the size of a 55-gallon drum (approximately 208 liters) to pass through. Private Prissy cautiously entered, finding herself in a much larger space. About ten meters away, an object lay slumped in a corner. With her long WOL drawn, she carefully approached. To her surprise, it was The Enac Supreme. "Are you hurt? Can you walk? How can I assist?" she asked urgently. The Enac Supreme, in a weak voice, responded, "I'll recover if I can get some dark life vegetation." Without hesitation, Private Prissy retrieved some dark life vegetation and handed it to The Enac Supreme. Miraculously, within minutes, the Enac Supreme regained strength and stood up. Private Prissy helped Enac Supreme out of the hidden space, as they began the climb back to the crater's rim.

Upon reaching the top, Private Prissy and The Enac Supreme rejoined the other crew members, who had gathered around The Ma'am as she attended Sergeant Waddles. General Boxdale quickly briefed The Enac Supreme on their encounter with Enac Grand and sought guidance on their next steps. The Enac Supreme, now fully recovered, said, "If you turn Enac Grand over to the Enacamytes, it will be confined according to our cultural practices." Following this advice, we handed Enac Grand over. As we descended Moonara, we turned over the other captured Enacamytes to The Enac Supreme as well and headed for Camp Salute. What an eventful few days it had been, I thought. But the best part was that hostilities had been averted. We were all tuckered out. To my knowledge, we all slept soundly that night.

Chapter 18.
Homeward Bound: Problem Solved - Or Is It?

We are now just two days away from our long-awaited trip home. Sergeant Waddles is back at one hundred percent, and the Ma'am has long since fully recovered. The HARM is fueled up, and all systems are go. Most of all, we can't wait to tell MCC about the abundant food and water resources we discovered in our backyard.

Before our departure, The Enac Supreme requested a meeting with General Boxdale. General Boxdale visited The Enac Supreme and received some shocking news. The Enac Supreme revealed the existence of a species called the Kahzonees from Planet Kah, located in another galaxy we had never heard of. The Kahzonees have been kidnapping Enac children recently. The reason given was that the

Kahzonees could not replicate and find pleasure in terrorizing the peaceful Enacs. The Enac Supreme proposed that New Earth protect their species in exchange for as much dark life vegetation and purple freeze as needed.

The Enac Supreme also requested that Enac Bebe return to New Earth with The HARM crew as an Enacamyte ambassador, formally requesting the assistance sought. General Boxdale brought this information back to the crew and led a discussion. The only question we could answer was whether Enac Bebe could go to New Earth with us, as we had been unsuccessful in contacting MCC since almost the beginning of the mission. The Universal Council would have to decide whether to protect the Enacs in exchange for their valuable food and water resources. Even without the consent of MCC, without exception, the crew thought that we should allow Enac Bebe to go with us to extend the offer to New Earth decision-makers. After a lengthy discussion, General Boxdale agreed to allow Enac Bebe to travel back to New Earth with us.

Finally, after weeks of spacecraft repairs and preparation The HARM and its crew headed home with Enac Bebe aboard. None of the crew was particularly religious except for me. But as we hurtled toward New Earth's atmosphere at over 4,000 kilometers per hour and at my request, an ancient gospel song played over the onboard communications system. The lyrics echoed in the cockpit: "I love to praise Him, I love to praise, (chorus) I love to praise His Name." Again, "I love to praise Him, (chorus) I love to praise His name. He's my rock, my rock, my sword, and shield; He's my wheel, in the middle of a wheel; He will never, never let me down; He is the joy that I have found; hallelujah, (chorus) hallelujah, I love to praise His name."

Strangely, this song soothed us as the sheer G-force contorted our faces to an almost unrecognizable degree. NASA once called this moment "The seven minutes of terror." A collective sigh of relief swept through the cabin as we survived reentry. After the rough descent into New Earth's atmosphere, Rascal reported to General Boxdale, his voice tinged with concern. "Sir, there's something not right about Enac Bebe. It's been acting uncharacteristically since our journey back to New Earth began." General Boxdale's eyes narrowed. "Keep a close watch on it, Rascal. We can't afford any malfunctions now."

As we re-entered New Earth's atmosphere, a piercing red ray of light from Planet Moonara shot towards us, its crimson beam unwavering and targeted. This was the same ominous light we all noticed when departing on our mission. It seemed to pinpoint a critical location where our military arsenal was stored. Were the Enacamytes monitoring us from afar? Did The Enac Supreme harbor a more sinister agenda than it had disclosed? Was the ray a threat to New Earth's safety? And what about Enac Bebe? Was it sent here as a covert agent to gather intelligence on us?

Suddenly, our comms link crackled to life. The HARM re-established contact with MCC. General Boxdale's voice broke through the static, steady, and authoritative. " The HARM to MCC, over," he repeated, his tone betraying a hint of urgency. After a few tense moments, punctuated by static and silence, MCC finally responded. "Good to hear your voice, General. Welcome home." General Boxdale chose to withhold the details of our findings until he could report them in person at MCC. The news, both good and bad, was too significant to relay over a tenuous communication link.

All was eerily quiet aboard The HARM as we gently descended toward the Roshna Desert in the sub-Saharan desert for landing. The silence was heavy with unspoken fears and uncertainties. Like my crewmates, I was plagued by doubts about how the New Earth community would react to our return. Would they welcome us as heroes or condemn us for the secrets we might have uncovered? The answers awaited us on the desolate sands below, where our journey would continue amidst new challenges and revelations.

Chapter 19.
At Last - Home Again

As our spacecraft floated towards New Earth, anticipation gripped us. This wasn't the New Earth we had left over a year ago. Our reentry had veered off course, guided only by makeshift instrumentation. Despite the cloudy day, the contours of New Africa emerged distinctly as we descended. The sky wore a dreary, grayish hue, unusual for this region. Cold rain pounded against the windows, perplexing me. I wondered why it was raining in this part of the world. Drought had plagued this part of New Africa for decades. Later, I learned of a new phenomenon: the Atmospheric River. With a resounding thud, we landed on New Earth. Peering out, all I saw was wet, dark gray sand. Yet, we were alive. After traversing hundreds of light-years over many months, I silently thanked almighty God for keeping us safe. General Boxdale initiated a welfare check. Each crew member responded with their last name, confirming our survival. With a collective sigh of relief, we knew we had all returned unharmed.

"Our first priority," General Boxdale declared, "is to meet with MCC after the debriefing protocols." We untethered ourselves, shedding our space gear and adjusting to New Earth's full gravity within the confines of the spacecraft. Over the next twenty-four hours, we gradually regained our balance and coordination. General Boxdale instructed Sergeant Paw, Rascal, and me to venture outside for a brief reconnaissance mission to assess the current situation firsthand. As we stepped out of The HARM, Sergeant Paw immediately queried Rascal, "Why is the sky so strangely tinted? And why is it rainy and cold in this desert?" Rascal paused momentarily, processing data from its memory banks before responding. "Radiation exposure aftermath," Rascal began, its synthesized voice clear despite the chaotic weather. "Five simultaneous nuclear reactor explosions, which triggered an underground thermonuclear bomb explosion, right after our departure; and injected particles and soot into the stratosphere, blocking sunlight. Temperatures have plummeted globally since that incident occurred. This atmospheric upheaval has worsened our already critical food and water shortages. The ozone layer depletion has continued to emit harmful sun rays, while an

Atmospheric River amplifies the downpour—a nuclear winter scenario to be exact."

Sergeant Paw gestured to retreat; concern etched on his face. "Let's return to The HARM immediately. We need proper protection from radiation." I nodded in agreement, and we hurried back inside. Rascal briefed the crew on the situation, prompting Sergeant Paw and me to put on our standard-issue PPE. Sergeant Paw secured his battery-powered APR (Air Purifying Respirator), while also suiting up in additional gear to shield against external contaminants and the harsh cold, providing a protective barrier against his skin or clothes from touching radioactive particles. Being a Brill, Rascal was naturally immune to these environmental hazards—an advantage that wasn't lost on him, as he expressed sympathy for our predicament. He reminded us that the current annual adult exposure limit to radiation was 2,000 millirems.

Equipped with an Airborne Contamination Monitor (formerly known as a Survey Meter or Geiger counter), tucked safely in Rascal's backpack, the three of us departed The HARM once more. Stepping out of the landing pod, we found ourselves navigating through slushy pools of rainwater atop the sand—a phenomenon I had never witnessed. Taking to the air briefly to assess our surroundings, I beheld a vast expanse of sand dunes stretching endlessly before us. The fallout had cast a dark, grayish hue over the landscape, reminiscent of the lifeless planets we had encountered on previous missions. The cold rain saturated my wing feathers, dragging me down like a plummeting comet. I trudged back to reunite with Rascal and Sergeant Paw. The topography here was very different compared to when we had set out on our mission. Rascal was wrapping up the first radiation check as I returned, the meter displaying a mere 350 Millirems—negligible, no need for protective gear here.

We regrouped at The HARM. Inside, Sergeant Waddles informed us that General Boxdale had reached out to MCC with new orders, summoning us promptly for a briefing. In the navigation compartment, the entire crew awaited General Boxdale's arrival. When he appeared, his voice echoed with urgency, "As you all know, MCC has made contact with us for the second time since our return to New Earth. They've been trying to reach us as fervently as we've been trying to reach them. Initially, they feared The HARM was lost to the nuclear blast upon departure. Learning of our safe return, MCC is dispatching an extraction team immediately to secure our position. The MCC itself had to relocate underground after the catastrophic event during our departure, which caused the communication blackout with The HARM." "Did you inform them about the discoveries on Moonara? The resources?" The Ma'am asked. General Boxdale faced The Ma'am with a knowing smile and said, "Not explicitly, but I hinted at the good news," Boxdale replied, eyes twinkling. "We're due for a joint debriefing after we clear health and environmental protocols." Sergeant Paw chuckled and said, "Boy are they in for a big surprise."

Se-rye, an uncommon attendee, spoke up eagerly, "General, when will they arrive? I miss my friends." Her question broke the room into laughter. "Soon, sweetheart," General Boxdale assured her, a warmth in his voice that mirrored Se-rye's beaming smile. Later that day, news arrived: a military carrier group positioned in the Indian Ocean near southeast Africa would retrieve them within 24 to 30 hours. Excitement filled the air as preparations for departure began. Rascal lightened the mood with his usual jests. "Why did Planet Moonara skip dinner? It was full! And why are stars bad at staring contests? Because they're always blinking!"

It was departure time and with anticipation and a mix of emotions, the crew gathered, each with a bag in hand, waiting for the approaching Chinook helicopters. Sergeant Z kept Lieutenant Jancedar close, while Enac Bebe and Rascal bantered nearby, their camaraderie evident. Suddenly, Se-rye's voice rang out, "They're coming!" Her excitement was contagious as two Chinooks thundered overhead, touching down with precision. A naval officer approached, saluting General Boxdale. "Welcome home, sir, to you and your crew." Returning the salute, the General spoke for them all, "It's good to be back." They boarded, escorted by military personnel securing The HARM. The officer in charge informed us that we were being transported back to his Carrier in the Indian Ocean, destined for a secure underground facility in New North America.

Upon arrival at the Carrier, the Commanding Officer warmly greeted us on the flight deck. After being fed, we were placed in isolated berths for quarantine, provided with PPE, and instructed to wear it for our upcoming journey the following morning. Exhausted, we slept soundly through the night. The next morning, we enjoyed a hearty breakfast before boarding an aircraft bound for New North America. Settling in for what would be a thirteen-hour flight, we were treated with utmost care despite the long journey. As we descended, the rugged contours of Utah's landscape came into view. It struck me how close we were to BSP. Touching down, we were shuttled by bus into the side of a mountain. The interior resembled a medium-sized city, albeit with shorter buildings and a pervasive military presence. After a brief journey inside, we halted, instructed to gather our belongings and follow our escorts. Enac Bebe and Lieutenant Jancedar were led to a separate holding area.

Chapter 20.
The Debriefings

G uided to a small, enclosed room, we were directed to put our gear on the floor and take a seat. Complying, we took our places, the tension was palpable among us. To our surprise, General Verdy from our initial launch entered the room. We instinctively stood at attention, but he quickly motioned for us to sit back down. His presence carried an air of authority and familiarity, instantly grounding us. "Ladies and gents, welcome home on behalf of a grateful planet," he began, his voice resonating with sincerity. "Each of you will be debriefed individually after completing your health and environment protocols. You will now be escorted to your respective protocol and debriefing areas." We were swiftly separated and led to different rooms, each step taking us further from the camaraderie we'd built on our mission. Two days of relentless poking and prodding passed before my debriefing time arrived. I was oblivious to the fact that

General Boxdale had already been questioned extensively before me. Oddly, they had not asked me anything about the food or water we had discovered, which struck me as peculiar.

When I was finally ushered into another room, General Boxdale, and five stern-faced debriefing officers awaited me. They explained they wanted to interview us together since General Boxdale had been temporarily incapacitated, and we were the two highest-ranking officers on the mission. The first question pierced the silence: "What was the most gratifying thing to you about the mission, and why?" Without hesitation, General Boxdale responded, "There were two things, not one. The discovery of life on another planet and the discovery of viable, long-term food and water sources. Right in our backyard." His voice carried a blend of pride and relief. I nodded in agreement. "I would agree," I added, feeling the weight of our discoveries.

Question after question followed, each probing deeper into our experiences and findings about those two monumental subjects. Hours passed as General Boxdale and I recounted every detail, our words weaving the narrative of our journey. It became clear why I had not been asked about food and water in my solo interview. The importance of our discoveries demanded the collective insights from both our perspectives.

The next day, we returned to continue the interview. As the session wrapped up, General Boxdale inquired whether Enac Bebe had been interviewed yet and learned it had not. General Verdy then instructed that General Boxdale be present for that interview. General Boxdale requested that Rascal and I join for language translation, which was approved.

The following morning, General Boxdale, Rascal, and I accompanied three officers to Enac Bebe's holding area. Upon entering, Rascal greeted Enac Bebe, who appeared visibly nervous and frightened. Despite the tension, Enac Bebe agreed to cooperate fully. It had been tested two days prior, but the DNA results were inconclusive. We reassured it, recalling the care we had provided on Planet Moonara, and mentioned we would administer something to ease its nerves. We transferred the liquid contents of an energy pack from a WOL into a vaccine vial and administered it. Enac Bebe visibly relaxed, and the interview began in earnest. Immediately, Enac Bebe began laughing uncontrollably. We secured it in a chair for questioning. The three officers surrounded Enac Bebe, their expressions stern. "What is your name?" one of them asked. "Bebe," it responded. "Where is your home located?" asked another. "A dark place away from here," it replied. "Why are you here?" a third officer inquired. "For the adventure of being in another place and to help my grandpa," Enac Bebe answered. "Who is your leader?" the first officer questioned. "My grandpa," Enac Bebe said. "You don't come to do us harm, do you?" the second officer asked. "No," Enac Bebe replied. "Does your grandpa want to help us?" asked the third officer. "Yes, for making me better," Enac Bebe answered. "How many of you are there?" the first officer continued. "Many, many," Enac Bebe responded. "Who are your new friends where you are now?" the second officer inquired. "The one you call Rascal and the one you call Jancedar. They are what you call nice to me and talk to me much," it replied. "You don't know how old you are, do you?" the third officer asked. "Not know what you mean," Enac Bebe said.

The questions went on for hours. Enac Bebe was eventually given a shot of the WOL antidote, making it fall asleep. At that time, we didn't know that the Enacamytes' DNA would allow it to lie, even with the laughing energy pack being administered. It had been a long day for all of us. As we were being escorted back to our living area, General

Boxdale and I had a chance to talk privately. He revealed that during the debriefing with Lieutenant Jancedar, he learned that while confined to quarters on Planet Moonara at Camp Salute, she had befriended Enac Bebe. Enac Grand discovered their friendship and used it to manipulate Enac Bebe into learning more about New Earth and us. Also, that Enac Grand aimed to prevent The Enac Supreme from allowing the New Earth species to access the dark life vegetation and the purple freeze. What Enac Grand truly wanted was to seize leadership of the Enacamytes. Lieutenant Jancedar further confessed that The Enac Supreme was unaware of her close relationship with Enac Bebe. She admitted that ambition, notoriety, and validation as a Pi-thar were what she sought, and she was willing to do anything to achieve them. That's why she was a stowaway on The HARM.

Chapter 21.
The Hunt

We had been back for about two weeks when we were informed that we'd be moving back to BSP. The facility had been retrofitted to handle the challenges of radioactivity. Our new assignment was to help prepare the Galaxy crew for what lay ahead on Planet Moonara.

Twenty-four hours before moving day, there was a knock on the door. It was General Boxdale. His expression was grave as he informed me that Lieutenant Jancedar and Enac Bebe were missing from their holding areas. Lieutenant Jancedar had manipulated her security detail, obtained the key fob to her confinement door, and escaped. Before leaving, she unlocked Enac Bebe's door, and they both fled together. Enac Bebe managed to subdue the security detail during their escape by spraying them with green Slyme, incapacitating them. The entire MCC was put on lockdown until further notice. Despite a thorough search, there was no sign of them in the bunker, so we were allowed to move to BSP.

The hunt for Lieutenant Jancedar and Enac Bebe was on. Jancedar was in control, as Enac Bebe knew nothing about New Earth. How did they escape such a secure facility? Where could they have gone? What were their plans? How dangerous were they? What were the health considerations for them and anyone they came into contact with? These questions and more needed answers.

As The HARM crew gathered back at BSP, General Boxdale called a meeting in the Gathering Hall. It felt so good to be back in a familiar place. The other crew members shared the same sentiment. As we settled in, Rascal cracked a joke, "How do we know that hot is faster than cold? Wait for it! Because you can catch a cold." Rascal and the rest of us burst into laughter. However, General Boxdale didn't join in. By the look on his face and his serious demeanor, something significant had happened.

He began talking about Lieutenant Jancedar and Enac Bebe's escape. "Does anyone have an idea where they might have gone?" Private Prissy responded, "Wherever they are, the Lieutenant must have led the way." We all nodded in agreement. The Ma'am spoke up, "I remember

Lieutenant Jancedar loved taking short flights to New Las Vegas, Nevada, whenever she could. It's not as glamorous as it used to be, but there are plenty of places to get lost or hide if you know what I mean. Maybe that's where we should start." "Alright, let's start there. It's only a few hundred kilometers from here," the General decided. He instructed Sergeant Paw, Rascal, and me to find them. "Sergeant Paw, take Rascal to the nanotechnology center to restore its remaining circuits before you leave," he added.

As we departed, I soared ahead to scout for Sergeant Paw and Rascal. My flight speed outmatched the vehicle transport, allowing me to provide effective surveillance. Wearing PPE goggles on our home planet felt odd, but like everything else since I left, I had to adapt. Approaching New Las Vegas, I noticed a commotion in the Voluptuous Sector, a part of the city infamous for gambling and other pleasures. Drawn by curiosity, I flew closer and saw an assembly of fire, police, medical, and hazmat emergency vehicles. I landed, flashed my credentials, and approached a law enforcement officer. "What happened here?" I asked. "A human female was taken into custody. She had no identification and refused to speak," he replied, pointing to a nearby woman. "Sector Chief Rocinda is in charge." I approached Chief Rocinda and showed her my credentials. "What's the situation?" I inquired. Her eyes met mine, and she began, "A female human at the Interstellar Craps venue was caught cheating by the AI. She became unruly, verbally abused the dealer, and slapped him. Security was called, and she was arrested. She's now in a sector patrol vehicle awaiting orders from the Sector Commander due to her military status." "Was anyone with her during the incident?" I asked. "Not that I'm aware of," she responded. "I need to speak with the Sector Commander immediately regarding interplanetary security," I insisted. She tried to contact him via portable communicator but received no response. I stayed nearby, waiting for an update. Meanwhile, I relayed my location coordinates to Sergeant Paw and Rascal.

Sergeant Paw and Rascal arrived just as we were waiting for the Sector Commander. I quickly filled them in on the situation. Soon after, the Sector Commander himself arrived. Detective Rocinda introduced us, and I explained who we were looking for and why. The Commander agreed to let us search the venue for the other party and assigned one of his officers to accompany us. Before heading to the Celestial Somnolence Hotel, I contacted General Boxdale for a status update. With a hotel staffer as our guide, we began our search for Enac Bebe. We warned the search party of the potential danger. We meticulously searched floor by floor, combing through both common areas and staff-only zones. When the staffer opened the door to the housekeeping linen closet, we found Enac Bebe huddled in a far corner, its single eye half-open, exuding fear and confusion.

Rascal approached cautiously, speaking softly to it. Almost immediately, he sensed something was off about Enac Bebe. Its eye widened as if recognizing a familiar face. Rascal performed a full retinal scan and confirmed our suspicions: it was an imposter. Drawing on my limited knowledge of the Enacamytes' language, Rascal gently asked the imposter how it was feeling and if it needed any help.

The imposter replied in a weary tone, expressing a need for dark life vegetation. Without hesitation, Rascal reached into his backpack, retrieved some dark-life vegetation, and handed it to the imposter. As soon as Enac Bebe's imposter took a few bites, the law enforcement officer burst into the room, his short WOL drawn. The imposter, feeling threatened, raised its arm and opened its mouth to fire, but the officer struck first. The imposter began to laugh maniacally as it fell to the floor, releasing sliyme from its mouth wildly, splattering the hotel housekeeper. The officer swiftly handcuffed the imposter as Rascal rushed to its side. I assisted the housekeeping staff and called for medical help. It all happened so fast. Rascal pulled Sergeant Paw and me aside, revealing the shocking truth about Enac Bebe being an imposter. I turned to them and said, "This changes everything."

General Boxdale arrived at the Celestial Somnolence Hotel, his face a mix of concern and determination. "Win, are you all right?" he asked. "Yeah, Tank, I'm fine, but I'm not sure about Enac Bebe. It's an imposter, and it took a nasty hit from a WOL. They're taking it for medical treatment now. Lieutenant Jancedar is over there in the law enforcement vehicle." I then filled in General Boxdale on all the details of the incident. "What a mess. We got what we did not want: an interplanetary incident, but we'll sort it all out," General Boxdale said with a sigh. He approached the Sector Commander, presenting digital documents from MCC, granting him jurisdiction over the incident.

General Boxdale, Sergeant Paw, and I followed law enforcement to the holding location for the Voluptuous Sector. Inside, I saw several Pi-thars in a containment area.

Lieutenant Jancedar was being unhandcuffed for processing when she suddenly lunged, grabbing Sergeant Paw's short WOL from his holster. She fired several wild bursts at us but missed. Sergeant Paw, along with several other officers, quickly subdued and re-handcuffed her. Throughout the chaos, Lieutenant Jancedar remained silent, her expression unreadable.

Chapter 22.
The Interviews

General Boxdale, Sergeant Paw, Rascal, and I headed to the local medical center's unit to check on Enac Bebe's imposter. The WOL's effects were still active. General Boxdale began the interrogation, "Are you the real Enac Bebe?" "No, I'm not, but I'm an excellent copy," the imposter replied. "Where is the real Enac Bebe?" General Boxdale pressed. "In a secret place," it responded. "Where specifically is the real Enac Bebe?" the General demanded. "In a secret place on The HARM," the imposter said. General Boxdale immediately halted the interview, exited the room, and called MCC. He requested The HARM be disassembled at once to locate the secret compartment where the real Enac Bebe was hidden. We returned to the room to continue the interrogation, but the effects of the WOL had almost completely worn off, so the interview was postponed. General Boxdale planned to resume it later.

Next, we went to Lieutenant Jancedar's holding area, hoping to interview her. Questions flooded my mind as we walked: Was the real Enac Bebe hurt? Did it survive the journey to New Earth? How would Enac Supreme react to the news of its grandson's imposter? Was our potential food and water resource agreement at risk? Would The Enac Supreme trust someone without an established relationship, like the Galaxy crew? General Boxdale coordinated with the Sector Commander to have Lieutenant Jancedar and Enac Bebe's imposter transported back to the BSP.

Lieutenant Jancedar was brought into the Debriefing Room at the BSP, where General Boxdale, Rascal, Sergeant Paw, and I were waiting. Given my training in Interrogation Extraction Techniques (IET), General Boxdale directed me to conduct the interview. Two short WOL bursts were administered to Jancedar to ensure her truthfulness. I began, "Is your real name Gloria Jancedar?" " No," she replied, causing our jaws to drop collectively. "What is your real name?" I pressed. "Tech Model JEC-AC TEN," she responded. "So, you're a Pi-Thar, 100% machine?" I asked, trying to wrap my mind around the revelation. "That is correct," she confirmed. We had been deceived and manipulated all this time. I continued with the questions.

"Do you have a gambling habit?" I inquired. "Yes," she responded. "Why did you take Enac Bebe along with you?" I asked. "I thought it might be useful to me," she answered. "In what way?" I prodded. "Using its weapon to my advantage," she said. "Are you sorry for what you did?" I asked. "No, only that I did not achieve my goal," she replied. "What was your ultimate goal?" I continued. "To be recognized as the one who brought food and water resources to New Earth, and to be famous," she admitted. "I should be recognized for being smarter than everyone else around me." After a series of probing questions, we took a brief break. When we reconvened for the second part of the interview, I turned to Lieutenant Jancedar and asked, "Are you angry with anyone or anything?" "Yes," she replied curtly. "Who are you angry with, and what is the reason?" I pressed. "I'm angry with the MCC for confining me during most of the HARM mission," she answered. "And I'm also angry with the The HARM crew—except for The Ma'am—for carrying out the mission without me." "And what do you think your punishment should be?" I inquired. "None," she said firmly. "I believe I should be set free because my purpose was noble."

After addressing several more questions, I wrapped up the interview with three final inquiries. "Why did you leave who you believed to be Enac Bebe alone at the hotel?" "For its own good," she responded enigmatically. "Is there any person or animal you hold in high regard?" I asked. "Captain Strossenborg—The Ma'am," Lieutenant Jancedar said, with a hint of admiration in her voice. "She's my heroine." "If you were freed, what would you do?" I asked as a last question. "I'm not sure at the moment," was her final, ambiguous reply.

As the night grew late and exhaustion set in, General Boxdale decided to halt proceedings for the day. We agreed to resume by re-interviewing Enac Bebe's imposter in the morning. Early the next day, General Boxdale received urgent news: The HARM had been disassembled overnight by the MCC, revealing a hidden compartment containing the real Enac Bebe. The General was summoned to oversee the opening of the containment unit. He contacted me and requested that I accompany him.

Before heading to The HARM, we first returned to re-interview Enac Bebe's imposter. The medical staff administered an injectable energy WOL Pak into its arm. The effect was almost immediate, and the interview commenced. Once again, the General asked that I take the lead. I needed the imposter to talk, so I posed an open-ended question: "Explain how you replaced the real Enac Bebe during the journey from Planet Moonara to New Earth." The imposter began, "It was all part of Enac Grand's master plan. Enac Grand wanted Enac Bebe out of the way while he orchestrated the seizure of power. The real Enac Bebe was to be put in stasis aboard The HARM, locked away in a secret, temperature-controlled cargo hold that could evade detection by the ship's instruments. The purpose was to slow down Bebe's biological functions, preserving its physiological capabilities. Enacamytes don't believe in killing, so this would ensure no heir could replace The Enac Supreme as leader. Enac Bebe was supposed to wake up in exile on Planet New Earth, while Enac Grand would seize complete control of the Enacamyte realm. That's also why Enac Grand kidnapped The Enac Supreme—he believed Enac Supreme would never be found in the crater you call Mt. Moonara."

I pressed further, "How were you planning to return to Planet Moonara?" The imposter responded, "That would have been straightforward using the beam." "The beam?" I asked, intrigued. "Yes," it explained, "It's a stream of red light that allows us to teleport to any known location by breaking down our energy and reassembling it at our chosen destination. It's a simple process. We've been using it for eons. When Sergeant Paw repaired Rascal right after the crash landing on Planet Moonara, we were aware that some circuits remained unrestored. Thus, Rascal couldn't detect me. Enac Grand then replaced the real Enac Bebe with me as the imposter. While I was ostensibly assisting with Rascal's repairs on The HARM, I was also constructing a secret compartment unbeknownst to Rascal." "Can we delve deeper into how the teleporting process works later?" I inquired. "Certainly," the imposter replied. "Whenever you like."

We confronted Enac Bebe's imposter, demanding to know why it had fired its weapon at us earlier. Rascal translated the imposter's explanation: it claimed it had to make it appear as though it was defending Rascal from harm. When asked about its separation from Lieutenant Jancedar, the imposter recounted that she had instructed it to wait where they were, but it had panicked and fled into the housekeeping closet. We inquired whether all its species on Planet Moonara were like it, and the imposter replied that they were not. Each member of its species was unique, much like the diverse beings here on New Earth.

We then proceeded to the location where The HARM had been disassembled, stopping for a quick meal on the way.

Upon arrival, we found, the stasis container had been detached from the rest of the machinery. General Boxdale gave the order to open it. As the container's lid was lifted, a dense, white mist billowed out, dissipating within moments to reveal Enac Bebe lying motionless inside. To our surprise, its body was encased in what appeared to be a solid block of ice.

Rascal reached in, his hand brushing against the icy surface. "Don't worry," he assured us. "This isn't real ice. It's a chemical solution made of supersaturated sodium acetate and a preservation agent. When exposed to air, it rapidly solidifies, but it's actually warm to the touch."

I hesitantly reached into the container and confirmed Rascal's claim—the block felt warm despite its icy appearance. Enac Bebe was carefully extracted and placed on an examination table. Medical personnel began assessing its vital signs and informed us that it would take several hours for Enac Bebe to regain consciousness. General Boxdale instructed us to return the following morning.

The following morning, we arrived at the facility around 0800 hours. We were informed that Enac Bebe was awake and requesting something, though they couldn't quite determine what it was. Rascal, however, had an instinctive sense of what Enac Bebe needed and had brought along some dark life vegetation. As soon as Enac Bebe spotted Rascal, its excitement was evident, its eyes widened and it began speaking at a rapid pace. After Enac Bebe had eaten and conversed with Rascal for a while, it was time for the interview. A dose of energy pak WOL was administered to Enac Bebe. I started with a straightforward question: "What is your name?" "Enac Bebe," it replied. I then asked, "What do you remember about being kidnapped?" Enac Bebe's gaze grew distant as it recalled, "I remember the last few days of repairs on The HARM on my home planet. I was walking when something came from behind. I felt a covering placed over my head, laced with something that made me unconscious. The next thing I knew, I woke up in a strange place on New Earth." Rascal then filled in the gaps about what had happened since. Curious, I asked, "Why do you think someone would want to kidnap you?" Enac Bebe's expression grew serious. "That's an easy question. The Enacamytes are peaceful now, but we were once a warrior species from a warring galaxy. We were cruel and ruthless out of necessity until my great-grandfather introduced a new era of peace. We fled the conflict, and due to some mechanical problems with our carriers, we ended up on Planet Moonara. My great-grandfather believed peace was the answer, even though Enac Grand, who disagreed, felt we should have stayed and fought for our home planet. Enac Grand tried to undermine my great-grandfather and my grandfather to replace them as our leader. Since I was next in line to lead, Enac Grand sought to remove me from the equation."

I pressed on, "Can you explain the red light from Planet Moonara that was directed at New Earth?" "Certainly," Enac Bebe said. "The red light is our method of transport and communication. It allows us to move quickly over short distances and telepathically communicate across vast spaces. Planet Moonara is very close to your New Earth. The light also helps us gather and analyze languages. We have been doing it to your planet to assess any potential hostile intents, especially when unusual activity occurs, like recently. However, we haven't sent any of our species to your planet; we've only been collecting data. I'm honored to represent my grandfather, whom you call The Enac Supreme, by speaking with your Council. And I'm deeply grateful for your rescue." I continued to ask various questions, and Enac Bebe answered each one willingly. With the interview concluded, we wrapped up for the day.

Chapter 23.
The Imposter's Demise

I returned to my quarters around 2100 hours, preparing to unwind for the night when my communicator began flashing urgently. It was General Boxdale, his voice tight with urgency as he explained that he had been summoned to the Pi-thar containment site for an emergency. He was en route to retrieve Rascal and needed me to join them immediately.

We arrived at the containment location almost simultaneously, a trio of tense figures converging in the dimly lit corridor. We were led to the holding area where Enac Bebe's imposter was secured. There, sprawled on the cold floor, lay the motionless figure of the imposter. Rascal knelt beside it, taking quick readings. The result was clear: there were no vital signs. The imposter was unequivocally dead.

The initial assumption that WOL bursts from its arrest might have been the cause of death was quickly debunked. BSP medical personnel conducted a thorough examination and discovered that the imposter's body harbored a nanotechnology enzyme sensitive to New Earth's atmospheric elements. Although the real Enac Bebe is not a Pi-thar, we must remain vigilant for any similar adverse reactions from this atmosphere.

Now, the pressing questions loom: How will the real Enac Bebe and The Enac Supreme respond to this revelation? When should we inform the Planetary Council? Could this incident spark an interplanetary conflict with the Enacamytes? Should we discuss the matter directly with The Enac Supreme? Who should be tasked with delivering this news? Was the imposter part of Enac Grand's scheme to sabotage the potential food and water agreement between our species? General Boxdale decided that we would withhold this information until the upcoming Planetary Council meeting. For the time being, the imposter was secured in the same stasis container used for the genuine Enac Bebe's transport to New Earth. The Council will determine its ultimate fate.

Chapter 24a.
The Planetary Council

After a few days, General Boxdale, Rascal, and I returned to visit the genuine Enac Bebe. It was nearly fully recovered and in high spirits. "How's the food?" Rascal joked with a smirk. "As good as back on my home planet," Enac Bebe replied, referencing the dark life vegetation with a playful nod. General Boxdale's expression turned serious as he asked, "Are you ready to represent your species before our Council?" "Yes," Enac Bebe quipped confidently, "that's exactly why I was sent."

As we made our way to the Planetary Council meeting, I asked Rascal if he was feeling nervous. He shook his head, insisting he wasn't, but I couldn't miss the flicker of unease in his eye. Entering the grand chamber, I was struck by the sight before us: representatives from one hundred and fifty nations, both human and non-human, filling the room with an air of solemn anticipation. Their gazes were locked on Enac Bebe, their faces a blend of awe and disbelief.

We were escorted to the front, where the Council's leadership facilitator awaited us. With a commanding presence, she rose and addressed the assembly. "Friends and colleagues," she began, her voice resonating with gravity, "today marks a historic moment. We stand on the brink of a new era, having discovered that we are not alone in the universe. Before us sits Enac Bebe, the grandson of the leader of the Enacamytes, a species residing on the dark side of our neighboring Planet Moonara." Turning to Enac Bebe, she continued warmly, "On behalf of the nations of Planet New Earth, we extend a heartfelt welcome. May this encounter foster peace and cooperation, and may we uncover ways for our planets to mutually benefit." She then gestured for Enac Bebe to join her at the podium. Rascal, acting as interpreter, gently guided Enac Bebe by the hand toward the podium, where he would join the facilitator at the heart of this pivotal meeting.

At the podium, the Council Facilitator turned to Enac Bebe and asked, "Please, tell us about your species and how you came to inhabit Planet Moonara." Enac Bebe remained composed as Rascal began interpreting the request. With a solemn tone, Enac Bebe began, "I speak on behalf of my grandfather, the leader of my people. We have lived on the dark planet for eons—long before your 'Big Boom' on New

Earth. We originated from a distant star system, far from here. Our ancestors fled a galaxy rife with conflict. My great-grandfather, who now rests among the stars, sought a sanctuary of peace. Unfortunately, due to some malfunctions with our rovers, we accidentally landed on the dark planet. It was then we discovered your presence. We attempted to establish contact but were deterred when the Big Boom occurred. Since then, we've observed from afar. Our technology is more advanced than yours, but our goal is peace. My grandfather wishes me to convey this message. He also wants you to know that we can provide all the food and water you need. In return, we ask only a modest favor." As Enac Bebe finished, the entire assembly rose in applause. The sudden outburst startled Enac Bebe, prompting Rascal to explain the situation.

The Council leadership then requested a private meeting with MCC leadership, Enac Bebe, General Boxdale, Rascal, and me. When the meeting commenced, Enac Bebe was asked what the Enacamytes desired from New Earth in exchange for their resources. Enac Bebe clarified that they sought protection from the Kahzonees, a request similar to the one previously made by The Enac Supreme during our visit to Moonara. We were told we would be notified once the Council reached a decision. Special accommodation was arranged for Enac Bebe at the BSP. Rascal dedicated much of his time to keeping Enac Bebe company and ensuring its emotional security.

A week has passed since the Planetary Council's last communication. General Boxdale received word that the Council had tentatively agreed to The Enac Supreme's proposal and the terms set forth by the Enacamytes. The rapport established between The Enac Supreme, Enac Bebe, and The HARM crew had made a strong impression. Consequently, the Council requested that the same crew return to Planet Moonara to finalize the agreement. It believed that the sensitive task of explaining the death of Enac Bebe's imposter would be handled more delicately by those already known to the Enacamytes.

In response, General Boxdale called a meeting with the crew. He relayed the Council's request: "We're being asked to head back to Planet Moonara to formalize the Enacamytes' offer and work out the specifics. They also want us to extend an invitation to Th Enac Supreme to vIsIt New Earth." This news sparked a wave of enthusiasm among us. The prospect of returning to Planet Moonara was thrilling. Private Prissy, too, was excited about the mission, though her joy was tinged with sadness. Her niece,

Se-rye, would not be accompanying us this time, and Prissy needed to arrange for a reliable caretaker in her absence. On the bright side, this mission would be significantly shorter than the last one.

One by one, the General inquired about our willingness to join the return mission. Private Prissy was the first to speak up. "Count me in," she said with a determined smile. Sergeant Paw chimed in confidently, "I'm ready to go. The mission's goals align perfectly with our sustainability efforts." The Ma'am nodded thoughtfully. "I'm always eager to advance our food and water sustainability initiatives," she added. Sergeant Waddles leaned forward with a grin. "I'm game for any adventure. Plus, I'm one hundred percent recovered now," he declared. "Well, as long as my trusty WOL is by my side, I'll go anywhere," said Sergeant Z with a determined nod. I chuckled, adding, "Someone's got to keep the General and you lot out of trouble, so I don't have much of a choice. Count me in too," I stated. Rascal shrugged, a smirk on his face. "No choice for me either, but I'm up for it," he said looking upward. The room erupted in laughter, easing the tension. General Boxdale nodded approvingly. "That settles it then. I'll inform the Council and arrange a timeline for the mission and launch date with MCC." His voice carried a sense of finality, and we all shared a look of agreement.

Chapter 24b.
Meanwhile

T he time had finally arrived for Lieutenant Jancedar's court-martial, and the charges were severe: Aerial Offenses. The Ma'am had insisted on attending to offer her moral support and had asked me to accompany her. Though I'm not usually inclined to attend these types of proceedings—they tend to cast a shadow over my mood—my respect for The Ma'am however made me agree. As we entered the courtroom, Lieutenant Jancedar was seated at the defendant's table, flanked by her Judge-Advocate (Lawyer). She held a stoic demeanor, but when she saw us, her eyes softened with a look of gratitude and approval.

General Boxdale took the stand to provide testimony on how Lieutenant Jancedar ended up on The HARM mission. Despite knowing she had breached the Uniform Code of Military Justice, I couldn't help but feel a pang of sympathy for her. The Ma'am seemed to share my sentiment. The court-martial was slated to continue for several more days, but I knew I couldn't bear more than a single day of the proceedings. A few days later, it was confirmed: Lieutenant Jancedar had been found guilty and sentenced to ten years in the stockade at Fort Heavenworth. First, however, she would undergo six months of re-education training and receive DNA-altering injections—a requirement for her, given her Pi-thar heritage. The news was disheartening but, in some way, expected. She could be released in six to six and a half years with good behavior. I pray so, as everyone deserves a second chance, even rehabilitated Pi-thars.

Chapter 25.
The Journey Back

O n a brighter note, training sessions are in full swing. This morning, I encountered Private Prissy and Sergeant Waddles at the Aquatic Dome. "Hey guys, how's it going?" I greeted. "I'm fine, sir. Just getting in an early swim," Sergeant Waddles replied. Private Prissy, looking a bit stressed, said, "Actually, sir, I'm feeling a bit overwhelmed. I'm searching for a reliable person to care for Se-rye while I'm away. We've interviewed four candidates so far." "It'll work out, you'll see," I reassured her. I then asked, "Is Captain Strossenborgg around this morning?" "Who?" Sergeant Waddles asked, looking puzzled. "Oh, I mean The Ma'am," I clarified. We chuckled, as her official title was rarely used. "She's in the water lab in the back," Private Prissy directed. I headed back to check on her, hoping to gauge her readiness for the upcoming mission.

The crew embarked on an exciting field trip to inspect our new spacecraft and assess its launch readiness. This upgraded vessel is a significant improvement over the original. Officially named The HARM II, it continues the legacy of the original Human and Animal Resource Mission (HARM). Touring its interior was nothing short of awesome. From what we saw, the atmosphere was brimming with optimism.

The HARM II boasts Pulse Propulsion Nuclear Engines, propelling it at twice the speed of its predecessor. Its features include a small detention room, a fitness area, an enhanced six-tier light and heat shield, and a well-equipped weapons compartment. The navigational telemetry has been upgraded to cutting-edge technology, and there's a full-service laboratory for specimen analysis. There are also two hideaway escape pods alongside the cargo bay to accommodate the entire crew plus one. The spacecraft is approximately one-third larger than the first HARM spacecraft. Notably, it also houses an onboard AI Brill, affectionately called Alice. Stationed permanently on the spacecraft, Alice performs all the functions that Rascal can, plus a few extras. Rascal, a Brill himself, is not pleased with Alice. He thinks she will replace him. His jealousy of Alice has sparked an AI rivalry already that promises to be intriguing.

It's launch day and the crew has boarded The HARM II. As the countdown ticked away, my heart fluttered with mixed emotions of anxiety and anticipation. Seated vertically atop the nose cone, I felt the powerful engines roar to life, lifting us from the surface. In an instant, it seemed we were a full kilometer above New Earth. General Boxdale eagerly anticipated his meeting with The Enac Supreme. Private Prissy wore a melancholic expression, missing her niece, Serye. Sergeant Z expressed his hope that the death of Enac Bebe's imposter wouldn't cause any fallout. Meanwhile, Sergeant Paw was relishing every moment of the journey.

On another note, Rascal relayed that Enac Bebe had been in contact with his grandfather, The Enac Supreme, via the "Red Beam," as the Enacamytes referred to it. The Enac Supreme was overjoyed to welcome us back to its home planet. However, Enac Bebe remained unaware of the imposter's demise. General Boxdale intended to personally deliver this grim news to The Enac Supreme.

It's day two of our mission, we were deep within Planet Moonara's orbit. As usual, The Ma'am was busy in the food and water lab, experimenting with a batch of Purple Freeze.

Sergeant Waddles was reviewing a munitions manual; and I was gazing out the porthole in my quarters, marveling at the heavenly works of God - what a breathtaking view! Sergeant Z made his way to the cargo bay for his routine security check. To his surprise, he detected unusual activity around the container holding the body of the deceased Enac Bebe imposter. Upon closer inspection, the readings from the container revealed an astonishing discovery: registered life activity. Without delay, he reported the situation to the General. Given our field medical training, Private Prissy and I were summoned to the scene. Upon our arrival, the General gave the order to unseal the container.

What we uncovered was nothing short of shocking. Inside, we detected a faint but unmistakable heartbeat. The imposter began to move its head slowly from side to side, its eye fluttering open. Its arms, sluggish at first, eventually stretching out. Rascal was called in as an interpreter, should the need arise. The containment unit was then relocated to the confinement area.

As day two drew to a close, General Boxdale summoned me to his quarters. "Win, I'm going to be direct," he began, his voice grim. "Your wife, Saba'ta, was found unconscious this morning. She's been rushed to a medical facility and is seriously ill. I don't have further details at this time, but I'll inform you as soon as MCC provides more information." A chill ran through me. "I had a premonition something was amiss right before we launched. I need to go pray. Excuse me, sir," I said, struggling to keep my composure. "Understood," the General replied solemnly. I retired to my quarters for the remainder of the day.

The following morning as we approached Planet Moonara's orbit, a peculiar sensation stirred in the pit of my stomach—an unsettling feeling I couldn't quite place or shake. Everything seemed normal, and our trajectory remained steady. As we prepared for descent, The HARM II's laser cannons were primed and ready, a precautionary measure given the potential threat posed by the Kahzonees. Peering through the porthole, I saw an alarming sight: a vast, light pinkish plume that stretched at least a kilometer high and as far as the eye could see, advancing towards us. There was no escape from it. Our only chance was to land The HARM II before we were consumed by the approaching mass.

Chapter 26.
The Landing and the Confrontation

B ased on our previous mission, returning to Planet Moonara felt like a sprint of a hundred meters. We were already in Moonara's gravitational orbit, slowly being pulled toward it. Landing approaches are always nerve-wracking, though we all kept our composure. A pink fog shrouded The HARM II as the spacecraft veered to port while entering Moonara's atmosphere. After what I would describe as a free-fall, The HARM II righted itself. Our speed dramatically decreased, and the thrusters' roar grew louder. Visibility was poor due to the pink fog, but the instruments reassured us that, despite the altered landing coordinates, we were still on target. I felt the parachutes deploy, and the noise of the thrusters diminished as we seemed to glide gently toward the surface. After a few minutes, a distinct thud signaled our touchdown on

Moonara's surface—yes, on the dark side, just kilometers from the Enacamytes' habitat.

As we touched down, a sense of tension crackled through the air. Sergeant Z headed straight for the weapons compartment, issuing each of us a long WOL, a short WOL, three energy packs, a handheld mobile laser cannon, and a shoulder harness with a belt holder. General Boxdale gathered us and said, "Soldiers, we don't know what we'll face out there, but we are prepared. Our mission is to ensure no casualties on either side. Set your WOLs to 1k kilojoules, per regulations; a 3k setting will be used only on my command. Understood?" We responded in unison, "Yes, sir."

Enac Bebe could hardly contain its excitement. It jabbered a mile a minute to Rascal, who struggled to keep up. "I'm home!" Enac Bebe exclaimed. Rascal, trying to lighten the mood, asked, "So, who's up for pizza, dine-in?" Laughter erupted among us, with Rascal leading the charge. General Boxdale decided we'd wait until the following morning to disembark. This would give the fog a chance to clear. He instructed Rascal to let Enac Bebe contact its grandfather, The Enac Supreme, to inform him of our arrival.

The next morning, the usual security landing party put on their PPE. Our team included Sergeant Z, Sergeant Paw, Rascal, Enac Bebe, and me, equipped with long and short WOLs. The Ma'am and Sergeant Waddles remained on board The HARM II, along with the confined Enac Bebe imposter. As we exited The HARM II, we found the fog still thick and unyielding. I had to fly my reconnaissance mission at a much lower altitude due to the poor visibility. While the ground crew began their trek toward the Enacamytes' habitat, Long WOLs held at the ready, I took to the skies.

The pinkish mist around us began to thin. We had covered about a hundred meters when I saw them—emerging about fifty meters directly in front of us. I spotted them at the same moment as the ground crew. As we communicated about the unexpected development, the ground crew halted. I joined them. Suddenly, Enac Bebe cried out in an excited state, "Oh, it's coming again, it's coming again! "

They were unlike anything we'd ever encountered. These beings, numbering in scores, stood between half a meter and a meter tall. Their rotund bodies were adorned with large, oval-shaped heads crowned with two pointed, unicorn-like horns. These horns, about fifteen centimeters high, flanked the top of their heads. Their mouths, shaped like interlocking stalagmites and stalactites, were filled with jagged teeth. Slanted red eyes, set against black glassy pupils, gazed at us as if in a trance. They had no visible ears, and their orange, shaggy bodies, streaked with intermittent black stripes, almost brushed the ground. No arms, hands, feet, or legs were visible. Their entire bodies seemed to pulsate with each breath they took. We later named them "Shags," based on their peculiar appearance. There we stood on the dark side of Planet Moonara, facing a mysterious species whose intentions were as enigmatic as their appearance. Were these the Kahzonees the Enacamytes had warned us about, or were they something entirely different? Were they hostile? Where had they come from? And did the Enacamytes know they were here?

There we stood, through the fog, face-to-face with these enigmatic beings, only about fifty meters apart. Neither side knew the other's intentions. The air was thick with tension. Were we on the brink of another interplanetary conflict, or was there a chance for peace? The fate of Moonara hangs in the balance. Will our heroes forge a path to understanding, or will they ignite a conflict that could alter the course of interplanetary history? The answers lie just beyond the fog.

Don't miss the thrilling continuation of this epic saga in "The Moonara 7: Planet of Plenty (Chapter 27)". The adventure is far from over—join us as the mystery unfolds and the stakes rise higher than ever before. Mark your calendars and get ready for the next chapter of this pulse-pounding journey!

9 798330 521937